THE MASTER CRIMINAL

By J. Jefferson Farjeon

Spitfire Publishers

D1523348

First published in March 1924 by Brentano's, London and later in 1924 by the Dial Press, New York. This edition published by Spitfire Publishing LTD. © Spitfire Publishing LTD, 2020

CONTENTS

ABOUT 'THE MASTER CRIMINAL'

A criminal gang responsible for half the organised crime in England is hunting for a stolen ruby of phenomenal value. But the kingpin behind the criminal syndicate is in fact an imposter. Can Scotland Yard's Inspector Mordaunt recover the stolen gem?

About the Author

Joseph Jefferson Farjeon was born into a literary family in Hampstead, north west London in 1883. He was a prolific crime writer, writing over sixty novels over the course of thirty years, many published by William Collins, Sons and featuring in their hugely popular Collins Crime Club. Dorothy L. Sayers said of his work, 'every word is entertaining.' His best-known novel (and play) *Number 17*, was made into a film by Alfred Hitchcock. He died in 1955.

Praise for The Master Criminal

'A terse, telling style... Farjeon displays a great deal of knowledge about story-telling'
New York Times.

'A Sherlock Holmes novel of the first degree'
New York Post

'An exciting, unusual detective story'
Wisconsin Library Bulletin

Praise for J. Jefferson Farjeon

'Jefferson Farjeon writes thrills enhanced by good writing, good humour, and good character sketches'
The Sunday Times

'This delightful writer delivers the goods once again'
The Daily Herald

'Mystery in White is the perfect book for a winter's evening, a cosy chair and an open fire'
The Daily Mail

'An undiluted joy... Ben is the plum of the book; his personality impresses itself upon the imagination'
Liverpool Post

'A top-hole thriller by a writer who knows his job'
The Daily Express

'Jefferson Farjeon is quite unsurpassed for creepy skill in mysterious adventures'
Dorothy L. Sayers

CHAPTER 1

An elderly gentleman, with silvery locks and genial eye, walked briskly along the sandy, dusty road that led from the sea to Woburn Station. He hummed softly to himself as he went, and looked neither to right nor left. Apparently, he had no single care in life, and considered the world a very pleasant place to live in.

But his unerring instinct told him that he was being followed, which explains why he looked neither to right nor left, and hummed so sweetly. Early in his career, John Mordaunt had learned the simple beauty of doing what was least expected of him. When danger threatened, he took no apparent notice of it. When it came, or grew into a certainty, he walked straight up to it, laid hold of its beard, and pulled it off. This principle, from which he rarely deviated, as rarely disappointed him.

The feeling that he was being followed annoyed him today. As a rule, he accepted such incidents with a serene placidity quite unnerving to his pursuers, who were as natural to him as was his own shadow. More than once they had tracked him across a continent, without obtaining any satisfaction for their pains. But this morning John Mordaunt determined to make a speedy and definite end to the pursuit, and the sweetness of his humming was the measure of his determination. Hitherto he had regarded himself as immune in Norfolk. Moreover, the day was an important one.

For some five minutes, he held steadily on his course, occasionally slackening his pace imperceptibly, and keeping his uncanny ear in tune. At last, when he had satisfied him- self that his suspicions were not groundless, he turned round abruptly, and swung back along the road over which he had just come. After a dozen yards, he swerved sharply to the left, stretched out a stick, and tapped the shoulder of a rough-looking fellow standing under a hedge.

"Ah!" he cried.

The rough-looking fellow, who had the appearance of a tramp, did not show any fear, but he looked a trifle uncomfortable. They made an odd pair as they stood on the sandy road, regarding each other. They were about the same height and build, but otherwise they looked as opposite as the poles.

"Now, then," exclaimed the old man, with a crisp note in his voice, "what's this for?"

"Wot's wot for?" replied the tramp, dully.

"Why have you been following me?"

"'Ave I been following you?"

John Mordaunt smiled.

"Don't let's waste time discussing an obvious fact," he observed. "Of course you've been following me. I want to know the meaning of it?" Suddenly he looked more closely at the fellow. "I've seen you before!"

"Yus," answered the man, heavily. "You give me a pound yesterday when I tole you my mother was ill in Bradford."

"I remember. And you nearly fell down in astonishment."

"They tole me you was a toff, but I never thought—"

"Yes, yes," interrupted the old man, a little testily. "We won't go into that. You're not a local man, are you?"

"No, sir."

"Well, don't you think it a strange way of showing your gratitude to dog my footsteps? If it's money you want, say so. I might spare you something."

"I ain't after money this time, sir," said the tramp, uneasily.

"No? Why, then we're back at the beginning again!" exclaimed John Mordaunt, tartly. "Why the deuce have you been following me?"

The man gave a quick look up and down the road before replying. Then he said, in a low voice:

"'Cos I ain't the only one. Young feller in light suit's on the same job. There's something up."

The old man considered the point. Then he spoke briskly.

"I appreciate your interest in me," he said, "but there's really no necessity for you to constitute yourself as my body-guard. I am very well able to look after myself. Very well able. I recall the man you're speaking of."

"Light suit," repeated the tramp.

"Yes, yes. And he's certainly been nosy this last day or so. I've not been blind to it. But why, in the name of goodness, should I worry about it? I haven't an enemy in the world. If I had, it might be different. Now, then, trot off. Oh, by the way—would you like another pound?"

A curious look came into the other's eye.

"No, sir," he mumbled. "I couldn't touch it. I ain't got a mother. That was a lie wot I told you."

John Mordaunt regarded him reprovingly through his gold-rimmed glasses.

"H'm," he said, shaking his head. "So you're a wrong 'un, eh?"

"Done a bit. But—" He hesitated.

"I knows a toff when I meets 'im. I'll see you don't come to no 'arm, mister."

"You would do me a favour by leaving me to myself," retorted the old man, briskly, as he turned on his heel and swung back again towards the station.

He did not look behind him to see whether the tramp was following or not, but walked, with determined haste, towards his objective. Once he consulted his watch, and increased his speed. The train was already signalled when he came in sight of the station, and he reached the platform just as the engine came round the curve.

The station-master saw him, and nodded respectfully.

"Only just in time, Mr Dicks," he said. "London express is prompt this morning."

The old man nodded back, and hurried to the little booking-office. Here he bought a first-class return ticket to Liverpool

Street Station, and, ten seconds later, he had selected an empty compartment in the comfortable corridor-train, and had sunk into a comer, with his small brown bag and stick by his side.

The station-master strolled up to the window for a brief chat.

"You're not deserting us for long, I hope, Mr Dicks? "he enquired, genially.

"I hope to be back in a day or two," replied the passenger, taking out a cigar-case, and opening it. "Have one? They're my specials."

"Thank you, sir. Very kind of you," exclaimed the station-master. He grew vaguely sentimental. "I reckon we miss you in these parts, when you're not here, Mr Dicks," he said. "You've been away too much lately."

"Tut, tut!" laughed the old man.

"It's true, sir. As the wife was saying only yesterday, when she saw the amount you'd given to the Lifeboat Fund—" His words trailed off, and he called out, in a stern voice, to a breathless figure approaching the platform:

"Stand away, there!"

The figure hesitated, and a porter ran towards him. He had neither luggage nor hat, and he looked slightly dishevelled. His light grey suit had a noticeable rent in it, while perspiration bore testimony to the obvious fact that he had been running.

After a moment's hesitation, he came on again. The train was moving, and the porter, glad to render any service to his Company when it lent him the assumption of authority, and reinforced also by the station-master's own command, obtruded his bulky form between the would-be passenger and the train.

"Let go!" shouted the young man, as the porter laid hold of him.

"Stand away there!" bawled the porter.

The train gathered speed. The porter's blood was up, and it was obvious that the young man had no chance.

John Mordaunt smiled as he watched the young man shake an impotent fist in the porter's face.

"By-laws must be kept," he murmured, whimsically. "And

there isn't another train for a couple of hours."

He took a newspaper out of his little brown bag, but it was evident that the news did not interest him greatly, for, after he had studied it for two whole minutes, he added: "And that's a local!"

The train churned its way through the flat lands of Norfolk and Suffolk, and made its usual substantial halt at Ipswich. John Mordaunt took advantage of the respite to stretch his legs on the platform, and, strolling up to a book-stall, enquired casually whether the London afternoon papers had arrived yet. The boy replied that they had not. The news must have been something of a disappointment to the old man, for he hummed contentedly as he returned to his comer seat. A minute later, the train resumed its journey.

John Mordaunt closed his eyes. The operation rested him without in any way detracting from his perception of what was going on around him. As his sense of sight was shut off, a new instinct was born in its place, safeguarding him as effectively through the darkness of repose. He knew, as plainly as though he had seen it, that his little brown bag was slowly slipping off the seat, and, without opening his eyes, he put his hand forward mechanically and saved it at the exact psychological moment. He knew, also, a few minutes later, that something unusual was happening in the corridor, and that the train was just passing over the flat marsh-lands where the Stour joins hands with the wide Essex estuary. He knew it, yet he did not open his eyes until the voice of the inspector gave him a logical excuse to do so.

"Is that the gentleman?" demanded the inspector, in a severe tone.

"Yus," came the response. "That's 'im."

John Mordaunt looked up blandly from his corner, and found himself being stared at by the ticket inspector and his old friend, the tramp.

"What's the trouble?" he asked the inspector, and then, turning to the tramp, added: "And how on earth did you get here?"

"That's just what I'm after finding out, sir," said the inspector, respectfully. "I'm very sorry to bother you, but this man's travelling without a ticket, and he says he hasn't got any money on him. He's given me the slip up to now, and I don't know where he got in—"

"Woburn, I imagine," interposed John Mordaunt.

"Ah, Woburn, was it? That's a tidy distance. He said you'd know him, and asked me to come along and find you. But, there, I don't suppose, sir, you want to make this your business?"

The old gentleman with silvery locks looked squarely at the tramp. The tramp looked at him, not quite so squarely. There was an uncomfortable gleam in the latter's eye which John Mordaunt did not fail to notice.

"And what makes you think, my man," he demanded, somewhat acidly, "that I am willing to act the Good Samaritan?"

"Wot's that?" said the tramp, stupidly.

"Why do you think I'll pay your fare?"

A faint, half-sheepish smile curled the tramp's mouth for a moment.

"That money you said you'd give me, sir— p'raps I'd take it now."

"Upon my word!" snorted John Mordaunt. Turning to the inspector, who looked somewhat mystified, he explained: "I met this fellow on my way to Woburn Station, and offered him a trifle, as he seemed in want. He refused. And now, it seems, he has changed his mind. What do you think of that for impudence? He thinks my heart is made of sugar!"

"Come along," said the inspector, putting his hand on the tramp's shoulder. "We've worried the gentleman long enough. I'll deal with you."

The tramp hesitated, and sent John Mordaunt an appealing look.

"Oh, very well," exclaimed the old gentleman, with humorous resignation. "I'll get the scamp out of his scrape. How much is the fare, inspector?"

"Seventeen shillings and twopence," answered the official.

"But, after all, sir, I don't see why—"

"Tut, tut! There's a pound note. You can keep the change. Oh, don't worry, I'm going to get my pound of flesh! If there's one thing I love, it's delivering moral lectures, and when you go I'll give this fellow the best moral lecture he's ever had."

"Thank you, sir," said the inspector, pocketing the note. He was about to depart, when he suddenly turned to the tramp. "And mind you hop out quick into a third-class compartment when the gentleman's finished with you. See?"

Outside, in the corridor, the inspector murmured: "Queer cove!" and beamed over his unexpected tip.

"Now, then," remarked John Mordaunt, when he was alone with the tramp. "Let's have the truth! Own up! I detest secrets."

The tramp's manner had undergone a subtle change. He was no longer the cowed creature he had been in the hands of the official. He became almost confidential.

"Remember that chap wot missed 'is train at Woburn, sir?" he asked.

John Mordaunt nodded.

"Quite well," he replied.

"That was the chap wot was following you. I made 'im miss 'is train."

"The devil you did!"

"Yus. 'E was up to no good, so I—tickled 'im up a bit, and then nipped in meself."

John Mordaunt regarded his companion severely.

"Do you know, you've done a very serious thing?" he exclaimed. "If I did my duty, I'd hand you over to the law for assault! That young man—"

"'E was following you, sir."

"Tut, tut! Haven't I already told you that I've no enemies? For that matter, *you're* following me, and, I tell you plainly, I won't have it. I don't like other people looking after me, however well-intentioned they may be. Now, listen. I don't want to seem unkind, but you force me to it. If ever I see your face again, I'll hand you over to the police."

"Orl right, mister. I'll keep off. But you're the first gent wot's ever given me a pound, and I ain't likely to forget it."

He turned, and went. John Mordaunt watched him go with a half-amused, half-quizzical expression. He considered the tramp distinctly interesting, and wondered whether he might not one day make use of him. And Fate, the impartial arbiter of our fortunes, hidden away in the mysterious realm wherein she dwells, found time to pause in her spinning and chuckle.

At Chelmsford two men got into the compartment. They thought the old man in the corner was asleep. But it was a common saying that this keen-brained individual never slept. He listened to their desultory conversation, and not until the squalor of London enveloped them, during the last ten minutes of the journey, were his pains rewarded. Then, indeed, an eyelid flickered.

One of the men was reading a paper—an early edition of the *Evening News*. Suddenly he observed:

"I wonder what the newspapers would do if there were no criminals in the world?"

His companion laughed.

"Well, we mustn't blame the newspapers," he said. "If we didn't read the stuff, they wouldn't print it. What's the latest?"

"Murder in Littlehampton."

"Anybody been detained?"

"Yes—permanently. They've shot the murderer." It was then that John Mordaunt's eyelid flickered. "Crime wave seems to be getting worse again," continued the speaker. "Do you suppose it means that morality, on the average, is lower—or that some devil of a genius for organizing criminality is at the back of it?"

"That's Geoffrey Mordaunt's idea, anyway," answered the other. "I've heard, from a friend of mine at Scotland Yard, that he's trying to track a big criminal who's at the bottom of most of these affairs."

"Who's that?"

"Can't say. Don't believe anybody can. Perhaps nothing more than a theory. When detectives can't find clues, they make them up eh?"

John Mordaunt smiled. It amused him that he should be regarded as a theory. The news that his brother was on his track did not worry him in the least. He had known it for years.

The train came to a halt in the super-gloom of Liverpool Street Station, and the two men alighted. John Mordaunt followed suit, after slipping the newspaper they had left behind them into his pocket.

CHAPTER 2

It was a brilliant, early-summer afternoon, and London was painted in gay colours, yielding its travesty of that beauty which no great city inherently possesses. Bright parasols and pretty dresses dotted the dusty streets, and there was an atmosphere of pleasant, conscious expectation, as though those within the pretty frocks were wearing them for the first time, and hoping for their due admiration.

At a corner of Oxford Circus, where the throngs were particularly thick, a girl who was innocently enjoying the happy pulsations of the afternoon received a sudden shock. A tramp blundered into her, sadly disarranging the primness of her blue costume.

For a moment, the tramp stared at her open-mouthed. Two weeks ago, he had played tennis with this girl. She was, in fact, engaged to him. But no recognition showed in her eyes, and the next moment the tramp had darted away again, while a cry of "Thief!" was raised on all sides.

A young man, flushed with anger and indignation, hurried by. "Yes, mine," he said, to an enquirer at his elbow. "There was eleven pounds in it." Then the crowds swallowed him up. Suddenly the crowds thickened at one spot, and eager hands seized a pale-faced, consumptive-looking individual.

"Caught you!" cried a triumphant voice. "No—that doesn't look like the fellow," came the high-pitched response of the victimized young man. Meanwhile, our tramp was jumping into a taxi up a by-street.

"Drive towards Langham Place like the devil," he commanded, in a sharp, authoritative voice, "and follow a taxi I'll point out to you. There's a five pound note for you at the end of it."

The chauffeur did not hesitate. The authoritative voice, and the golden promise, did their work. In a trice, they had flashed into Regent Street, sped by Queen's Hall, and entered the wide, straight stretch that leads to Regent's Park. The chauffeur nodded when his fare pointed out the taxi he was to follow, and settled down to his work with enthusiasm. Adventures did not often come his way.

The chase lasted ten minutes. It ended at a big shop, at the main entrance to which the pursued taxi had stopped. A tall, straight-backed man, with dark eyebrows and a heavy black moustache, got out, paid his fare, and entered the shop. The driver of the pursuing taxi pulled up some little way off, and asked for instructions.

"That's all," said the tramp, taking five pounds out of his pocket. He handed the money to the driver, dismissed him, and strolled towards the shop entrance.

The driver watched him curiously. He would like to have stayed, to witness the end of the episode, but another fare came along, and he was soon speeding back again towards the West End.

Meanwhile, the tramp investigated the shop, noted its two egresses, and hung around. He did not hide himself, excepting at one moment when he slipped up a back street, and, putting his hand to his hip pocket, traced the comfortable outline of a small revolver. He watched all the people who came out of the shop closely, and placed himself with marked conspicuousness before one or two. It was not until he had waited nearly an hour that a grey-haired, clean-shaven man emerged, and deigned to notice him.

It was the merest glance, but it told its story to the tramp. He touched his cap. The man walked on, ignoring him, and the tramp fell into step by his side.

"What do you want?" demanded the man, sharply.

"Ain't got no enemies, ain't you?" replied the tramp. "Then

wot d'you want to be a quick-change artist for?"

"I don't know what you're talking about!" exclaimed the man, angrily. "Be off, or I'll call a policeman!"

"It ain't no good, mister," said the tramp. "I knows you. I've been watchin' that shop, and no one like you ever went in."

The man began to walk towards a policeman, standing on a street island.

"Orl rite," mumbled the tramp. "But I wouldn't, if I was you."

"Why not?" demanded the man, turning.

"Becos' it won't 'elp you. I don't know wot game you're up to, sir, and I don't care. That's your business, not mine. But I've put two chaps off your scent today, and p'raps I'll be lucky with a third, Mr Dicks."

John Mordaunt looked at the tramp with a puzzled expression. His features relaxed slightly.

"What makes you think I am Mr Dicks?" he asked.

"Well," said the tramp, "as I didn't think I might reckonise you, I thought I'd let you reckonise me. See?"

"You're a smart fellow," exclaimed John Mordaunt, with a note of real admiration in his voice.

"I 'as to be," retorted the tramp, "I was nearly copped for a pickpocket at Oxford Circus, by a young chap wot never 'ad 'is pocket picked at all, I reckon. 'E must 'ave been another of them fellers wet's following you, and seems as if 'e didn't want me on the game too. But I leads the crowd up to the wrong man, and then 'ooks it. You see, sir, you ain't safe, and that's a fack."

John Mordaunt hesitated for the fraction of a second. Then he suddenly made up his mind.

"I'm going to ask you three questions," he said, "and, if your answers don't satisfy me. I'll hand you over to that policeman. How did you know the name of Oxford Circus?"

"Well, I've lived in Lunnon six years— I oughter know it," replied the tramp.

"How did you have the money to follow me in a taxi?"

"Ticket collector never give you no receipt, did 'e? No, 'e give me that arterwards, and made out as if I got in at Chelmsford. 'E was sorry for me, 'avin' nothing, and give me the difference."

"What swindlers there are in the world!" murmured John Mordaunt, "And, lastly, how did you learn all your clever tricks?"

"'Cos I'm a crook, mister," replied the tramp, "same as you."

"I accept the admission without the comparison," observed John Mordaunt, with a dry laugh. Then he called a taxi, and invited the tramp to get into it. The tramp hesitated for an instant.

"Wot are you going to do with me?" he asked.

"Save you the trouble of hanging on behind," replied John Mordaunt, blandly.

"I say, mister. You *are* a crook, ain't you?"

The question received no answer. The tramp found himself suddenly assisted in from behind, and the next moment his companion had jumped in beside him and the taxi was on its way.

Not a word was spoken until the journey was nearly over. Then John Mordaunt addressed the tramp, and his manner had perceptibly hardened.

"Now, listen," he said. "You have chosen to stick to me. You shall. And, so long as you stick to me, and all I stand for, just so long will I stick to you. But, if ever you break away now, your life won't be worth a second's purchase. Do you understand that?"

"Yus," replied the tramp, soberly. "Wot'll I 'ave to do?"

"Are you particular?"

"Not so long as you ain't. But you're my boss, and nobody else, see?"

"Whatever orders you receive will come directly or indirectly from me."

The taxi pulled up outside the tobacconist's shop opposite Notting Hill Gate Station. John Mordaunt paid off the driver, and then led his companion through devious routes to a large, sombre-looking house. He drew a key from his pocket, and, opening the door, shoved the tramp in ahead of him.

As John Mordaunt closed the front door behind him, the door of a room on the left of a dim hall was opened, and a woman came out. Even though the light was feeble, and appeared particularly so after the bright glare of the sunshine outside, the tramp could see that the woman's face was an unusually beautiful one, and that she moved with a lithe and sinuous grace. She raised her eyes enquiringly as she saw John Mordaunt's companion.

"This is a new recruit," said John Mordaunt, answering her glance.

"Indeed?" she murmured, with half-closed eyes, but, though they were half- closed, the tramp felt that they were piercing him through and through. "You think it wise?" she asked. Her voice was soft and rich, and she placed her hand on John Mordaunt's sleeve with a familiarity which had made many other men jealous, although he himself had never betrayed any special gratification.

"Wise? Have I ever done anything that was not wise?" answered John Mordaunt. "Or failed to turn a fact to good account? I did not bring this fellow along with me because of its wisdom, but because of its inevitability."

"Why was it inevitable?"

"Because he stuck to me like a leech, Beatrice, all the way from Woburn. We have got to deal with him—one way or the other."

Again the half-closed eyes were fixed upon the tramp, half-curiously, half-contemptuously. Then followed a brief, whispered consultation between her and John Mordaunt. The tramp stood, meanwhile, out of earshot.

Presently, beckoning to the tramp, the beautiful woman led him up a flight of stairs into a half-furnished room at the back of the house.

"Sit down," she said, "and stay here till you're wanted."

"Orl rite," answered the tramp. "Only I 'ope 'e don't keep me waiting long."

"Tramps can't be choosers," she retorted, rather curtly.

"That's rite, miss. It's the toffs git all the plums."

He looked at her hard, and she read his meaning. This did not diminish her haughtiness, but the tramp detected the vague unbending of a vain woman behind her slightly heightened colour.

"Why are you staring at me?" she demanded.

"'Cos you're beautiful," replied the tramp.

"Do you know you are very impertinent?"

"You wouldn't think it if I'd a stiff collar on and was clean."

"You're quite intelligent," she conceded, "for a tramp."

Responding to a momentary instinct—an instinctive, subconscious recognition of a fact denied to her intelligence—she smiled at him. For an instant, the brown eyes looked very soft beneath their crown of auburn-tinged hair. But the tramp's next remark was disappointing.

"Yes," said the tramp, "beautiful—and wicked."

An angry flush spread over her features as she turned, biting her lip, and walked to the door.

"Pity you couldn't 'ave made something better of yer life, miss," said the tramp.

She stopped, and turned round again. Whatever she may have felt, she answered coolly.

"I don't feel inclined to discuss my life with you," she remarked, with a smile that was no longer soft. "But perhaps you might have made something more of your own life?"

"Wot chance 'as a tramp?" enquired the man.

"I was a poor girl once. I made my chance. You, quite clearly, threw your chance away. I have no further interest in you."

"One minute, miss! D'yer mean you ain't going ter be my friend?"

"Come, come!" she responded. "I called you a man of intelligence just now. I retract. Is it likely that I should be your friend?"

The tramp nodded thoughtfully.

"And you never needed a friend," she added, "more than you do at this moment."

"Ah, I've got the one I need," exclaimed the tramp, shrewdly. "The man wot brought me 'ere. I reckon 'e'll see me through."

"You do? Well, I'll tell you something. You cannot remain his friend unless you are also mine. And it is quite clear you can never be mine. I don't like you, my good man. I don't trust you.

"Not trust me, miss?" The tramp's voice was deeply injured.

"Well, perhaps you're only a fool. Certainly, it was the act of a fool to come here today."

"P'raps you're right," muttered the tramp. "But, as I'm 'ere, it's no use frettin'. I say, miss—are you 'is wife?"

Something in the sudden intensity of the question made her reply, half against her will.

"No, I am not his wife—yet."

A look of relief spread over the tramp's face, which she was shrewd enough to observe, but not to interpret. His next words were almost light-hearted.

"Wot's all this about?" he asked. "Got a big job on?"

She left the room without answering. He heard the key turned after her.

For a few moments, he sat perfectly still. He stared at the ground, and his face took on an expression of great sadness. He smelt the elusive fragrance of the woman's presence, heard the echo of her rustling skirts; and then, suddenly, there came the vision of the girl he had encountered at Oxford Circus. Something very like a groan escaped him.

Below he heard voices. Sometimes they were soft and muffled, sometimes raised. Presently, rousing himself abruptly from his temporary inactivity, he groped about the room. He took its bearings, examined the window, and then turned back a comer of the carpet. A small crack was revealed in the wooden floor. He knelt down, and put his ear to it.

For half an hour he listened. Then he rose with gritted teeth, and a strange, strained look in his eye. The tramp seemed suddenly to have aged. Footsteps sounded outside, and the tramp knew that he was approaching the greatest crisis of his life.

CHAPTER 3

When Beatrice Fullerton re-entered the room which she had left on the arrival of John Mordaunt and the tramp, five men were awaiting her.

One of them—John Mordaunt—made no movement, but went on studying a newspaper report laid out on the table before him. The others all looked up, reflecting their pleasure in various ways. A big, boyish-looking man, with a face that would have been wholly benign but for his small, too narrow eyes, smiled frankly at her as she entered. Impatience was not among his weaknesses. He could wait a day, or a week, or a year, to achieve an end he had set his heart on, without betraying any evidence of distress. The tall, lank man who sat beside him, on the other hand, hated Time when it lagged, and grudged every minute that went by inactively. The glance with which he greeted Beatrice Fullerton told her plainly, because there was no attempt at concealment, that his nerves were on edge and that she had remained with the tramp too long for his liking.

A moody young man, a fit subject for a musical comedy hero but for a scar on his left cheek and an ugliness which was indefinable because it was not an ugliness of the face, but of the soul, showed almost equal relief, and expressed it in a sudden shedding of his moodiness. The last member of the party, a dwarf, merely grinned.

No one spoke for a few moments. They were waiting for John Mordaunt to finish his reading. Beatrice watched him with an inscrutable smile. Then, suddenly, in a sort of desperate defiance, not unlike the defiance of a bold child breaking a strict nursery convention, the tall man burst out:

"Well, well. Let's get on with it!"

John Mordaunt did not look up even then. The bold child found himself in the minority, and chafed all the more because Beatrice had transferred her gaze from John Mordaunt to him, and he did not like the quality of her expression. Thoroughly goaded—he had not slept for three nights—he fell back upon the consolation of a cigarette.

"You were a long time, Beatrice," commented John Mordaunt, when he had finished reading.

"I was having a heart-to-heart talk with your tramp, John," she replied. She laid the slightest emphasis on the Christian name, as though she enjoyed using it.

"What did you think of him?"

"Too intelligent," she said, bluntly. "I don't trust him."

"Nor do I," remarked the tall man. "Why did you bring him here?"

"Our friend, Mr Edward Tapley, has a wonderful faculty for piercing character through a closed door," remarked John Mordaunt, smoothly.

"Look here, we don't want any sarcasm!"

"There will be none, if there is no cause for it. How is it that you mistrust a tramp whom you have never seen, and about whom you know nothing?"

"I mistrust all strangers," growled the tall man.

"That is not necessary when I introduce them to you, perhaps," suggested John Mordaunt. "Otherwise, it's an excellent principle."

The big fat man came to his tall colleague's assistance.

"For my part, I never trust anybody in the world," he said in a high voice, which assisted his boyish atmosphere—his voice had never properly broken. "I don't trust a person in this room. I don't even trust myself. The only thing that holds us together —the only thing that holds the world together—is a common interest. If that goes—fizz!" He snapped his fingers, and chuckled. "And there's nothing so binding as a common discontent," he added. "That's why I'm all for unemployment, and why

I'm doing my level best to foster it. If you'll only bring your mind to bear on my little scheme, Chief, and organize it, we'll soon have the country ripe for any kind of coup we want to bring off.

"It's a sweet idea," said Beatrice Fullerton, "but aren't we rather off the track? We're dealing with facts at the moment, not theories—"

"But I want the Chief to make my theory a fact!" grumbled the fat man.

"All in good time, Tobias. Meanwhile, what about this tramp?" She looked at John Mordaunt. "What are you going to do with him?"

"What would you do with him?" asked the Chief.

"Shall I tell you. Honestly?"

"Of course."

"I'd get rid of him."

The dwarf guffawed. It was noticeable that the only person in the room who showed any repulsion for the dwarf was the tall, thin man. He shuddered slightly, a shudder of loathing rather than of fear, and found himself challenged.

"Really, Mr Tapley, you're most inconsistent," said Beatrice Fullerton, insolently. "We mustn't quarrel with our tools,"

Edward Tapley shrugged his shoulders. He realized that this was one of his off days. If only Beatrice Fullerton had been less beautiful, he told himself savagely, he would not have cared. The other people did not matter a rap—no not even John Mordaunt. But, even as he had that thought, he found John Mordaunt's piercing eyes upon him, and he knew that the Chief had planted fear as well as jealousy in his heart.

Unhappy though Edward Tapley was, the unhappiest man in that unhappy building was the tramp, listening upstairs with his ear glued to a crack. Every word shot through him with the agony of pain, and his face grew more and more haggard. He could not see the speakers, yet the voice and atmosphere of each conveyed their impression so vividly that he could almost visualize the scene which was so soon to find its termination in his own room. Sometimes it seemed as though he were listening in a dream, and that these creatures were mere figures of his imagination, wherein they indeed had figured for so many years. But he knew that this was merely the psychological pretence set up in weak moments by all who fear to face the truth—from the little child who pretends hard it is not going to have a tooth out to the strong man who denies that there is such a thing as Death.

"We will discuss the tramp presently," the voice of John Mordaunt was saying. "For the moment, I reserve judgment as to whether or not we shall be able to use him. If we cannot use him, we shall of course have to get rid of him. You can leave him safely in my hands. Now, Joe, let's hear your story, and don't make it a long one. Someone has bungled this Littlehampton affair, and I've got to put my finger on the weakness."

"Baxter was the weakness," said the fat man. "That's clear. And he's paid the price."

"So have we paid the price," interposed Edward Tapley.

"Well, we'll hear Joe's story," said John Mordaunt. "You got to Littlehampton, according to plan?"

"Yes, sir," said the dwarf, speaking for the first time. "Begun at Brighton, as you said, drawing pickchers in the sand. As you said. Worked along the coast through Shoreham and Worthing to Littlehampton. I'm there now. Leastways, will be again tomorrer. Drawing pickchers, as you said." He spat— a habit he could refrain from in company when silent, but never when he spoke. "Got the dates right and everything. Got the lie of the land. Old fellow's house three miles from the town. Just right. Got in through the winder. Easy. Big house. Only three in it. Fifty winders. No dog. Easy. Got in, and found him—"

"And killed him," said John Mordaunt. "It seems to me that you started the bungling, Joe."

"Had to kill him. No other way, sir. He was lookin' at it. £20,000, you said. Had to kill him. Well, didn't I?" The even tone became momentarily querulous. "Of course. No one spotted me. Easy. Got away. Went to the inn, as you said—"

"Ah, that was the mistake in the whole plan!" interrupted Edward Tapley. "I said so, all along. Joe ought to have brought the ruby straight to us."

"That's yet to be proved," answered John Mordaunt. "You give up too early in the game, Tapley. We will have that ruby yet. True, we're baffled for the moment, but so are the police. If Joe had kept it, he was a more likely character to be caught than Baxter."

"But Baxter bungled it," the fat man pointed out.

"That we admit," conceded John Mordaunt, "as Joe might have done had he not been instructed to pass on a jewel worth £20,000. Well, Joe, go on with your story."

"Went to the inn," resumed Joe, picking up the thread at once, "as you said. Found Baxter, fashionable-dressed, as you said, at a table. Took next table. Presently Baxter comes across, and asks for the salt. They was big salt-cellars, as you said. I passes him the whole cruet, and he takes it to his table."

"Of course, the ruby was in the salt?" queried John Mordaunt.

"Oh, no!" chuckled the dwarf.

"And you saw that it was quite covered?"

"Never know it. Smooth as snow. He leaves before me. That's all. This morning I got a wire at eleven. Sister ill. Took the 10.12. And here I am. All done, jest as you said.

There was a short silence. It was broken by John Mordaunt.

"Joe's narrative is merely the beginning of the story," he said, "I'll now read out the end of it, as given in the latest edition of the *Evening Standard*." He took up the newspaper. "The affair is given a good deal of prominence, and is headed:

"'Who killed James Cardhew?

Mysterious Tragedy on the South Coast.

Where's the Ruby?

"'Further details of the extraordinary murder mystery at Littlehampton, briefly reported in our earlier editions, have come to hand. The detective who had been shadowing Mr A. P. Smith —probably an *alias*—saw him emerge from a small inn named the Green Stag at about nine o'clock yesterday evening. He did not think this particularly significant at the time, for Mr Smith seems to have been a man of regular habits, and frequently had a late meal at this inn after a long country ramble and before returning to his rooms in Marine Row. But the detective's suspicions were aroused when he saw Smith take something covertly from his pocket, and look at it intently. He decided, from that moment, to watch Smith's every movement.

"'Smith went straight back to his lodgings and up to his sitting-room. The detective is positive that he did not leave the sitting-room from that moment until the moment of his own entry, an hour later, with other police officers, and this is corroborated by the landlady. The subsequent entry was effected in consequence of the news of James Cardhew's murder and the loss of the valuable ruby which he had recently received from Burma—a stone worth, it is stated, some £20,000.

"'Smith offered an extraordinary resistance. He was armed with a revolver, and fired three times, two of his shots wounding one of the policemen in the leg. He appeared to be cornered, when he managed to put out the light and jump out of the window. A chase lasting some ten minutes followed. In the end, the man was shot dead.

"'Those who made Smith's acquaintance at Littlehampton, where he was ostensibly on holiday, considered him a likeable man. His habits, as has been indicated, were regular, and he entered a little into the social life of the town. He was evidently a man of mystery however, and, if the police know anything about him, they are reticent to speak of it. That he was indirectly connected with the murder of James Cardhew seems probable, although there is no direct evidence of this. If indeed he possessed the ruby, he seems to have effectively got rid of it again. No trace of the missing gem has been found.'

"And that," concluded John Mordaunt, "is as far as the report goes, though I see in the 'Stop-press news' that the police have secured an important clue and hope shortly to make an arrest."

The dwarf did not look in the least perturbed. He imagined, indeed, that he bore a charmed life, and in this he was not so different from the majority of his fellow-creatures. We all of us live in the shadow of Vesuvius, yet cannot believe that the eruption will ever take place; but, as long as the steadiness of the world appears to depend upon blindness, true steadiness will never come. It may be said, however, of this particular scamp that he had some justification for believing in his immortality. He was one of the cleverest pawns in the kingdom of crime, and his manoeuvres were planned by one of the cleverest minds. But for this, his career would have ended many years previously.

"Am I to go back to Littlehampton tomorrow?" he asked, in a matter-of-fact voice.

"Your sister is better," smiled John Mordaunt. "It is quite safe for you to return."

"All right," said the dwarf. "But suppose they cop me?"

"A blow half-met is but half-felt. Your return to Littlehampton, coupled with the absence of direct evidence, will be all in your favour if you are arrested. And you may be arrested, in either case. You heard a lot of local talk this morning, of course?"

"There's no other subject," replied the dwarf, "in Littlehampton."

"Did they find Baxter's revolver?"

The question was asked so casually that Beatrice, who understood many sides of John Mordaunt's character, though not all, realized there was some special intention behind it.

"No, not yet," answered the dwarf. "They think he threw it away."

Beatrice watched for the flicker of John Mordaunt's eyelid; but he knew her even better than she knew him, and his eyelid told her nothing.

"And now what?" asked the fat man.

"I suggest that we let the matter rip," said the young man with the scar. It was his first contribution. He was a good listener.

"And lose £20,000!" exclaimed Edward Tapley. "The man's a fool. We've *got* to find that ruby. Confound it! We need money just now, if we're to get ahead. Do you realize the amount I've paid out in bribes during the past year? I tell you, if we're to hold together, we need money—and mainly because the Chief —" He hesitated, but plunged on, recklessly. Those three sleepless nights had told on him. "Yes, we need money because our Chief takes the lion's share, and never breathes a word of what he does with it!"

"It costs money to live these days," murmured the fat man, looking at John Mordaunt rather anxiously.

But John Mordaunt was quite unruffled. He remarked that any member of their organization was quite at liberty to leave them, if they did not like the terms—at their own personal risk. Edward Tapley suddenly crumpled up again, seeking consolation in the inevitable cigarette.

"Now, listen to me, all of you," said John Mordaunt, in a quiet, assured voice. "We are going to get that ruby, and I have very little doubt in my own mind where it is."

"The devil you have!" murmured the fat man, with genuine and generous admiration in his tone.

"I have not quite fixed on the plan, but probably I will go down to Littlehampton myself, with Beatrice. We may need the help of a third party. Joe would have done, but I am afraid his peculiarly delicate position rules him out. I will toss Joe pennies from the parade, but I will not know him."

"Will I do?" asked the fat man, benignly.

"You will not do," replied John Mordaunt, decisively.

"I'm in this, if I fit the part," said the young man with the scar.

John Mordaunt again shook his head. "No, the man I'm thinking of for the part is our friend upstairs," he replied.

"Be careful, John," Beatrice warned him. "I am some reader of character, you know. The man hates me like poison. I entirely failed to charm him."

"Then he, obviously, is no reader of character," observed the fat man. "If he had read you aright, how could he have failed to love our Beatrice?"

"Don't worry," said John Mordaunt. "If I'm not satisfied with him, I'll not take him. But a new ally would be useful just now—in case anything happens to Joe. This may be a way of testing our vagabond friend's good faith and efficiency. If he proves false, he shall meet the usual fate. That I promise you." He rose from his chair. "Wait, all of you, till I return. Don't grow impatient. The interview may be rather a long one, for I am going to leave no stone unturned, and, when I come back, there will be nothing about that tramp that I do not know."

"Don't be squeamish, John, if he gives trouble," said Beatrice, looking at him squarely.

He was walking towards the door. He paused at her warning.

"Have I ever been squeamish?" he demanded.

"No," muttered Beatrice. "Never. All the same, there's something about that tramp that worries me.

"Nerves, my dear, nerves," retorted John Mordaunt, smiling. And he left the room.

CHAPTER 4

John Mordaunt turned the key in the door, and, entering the room, found the tramp sitting in the chair in which the beautiful woman had left him. He locked the door again after him, and pocketed the key.

"Now," said John Mordaunt, "we can talk."

"Ah," replied the tramp, and waited.

"We have discussed your case very thoroughly," proceeded John Mordaunt—the tramp already knew that, for he had heard every word—"and, I must tell you quite frankly, my own inclination to give you a trial is not universally shared. But my word is law, and, if I feel satisfied after this interview that you mean to stand by us, I shall decide to put you to the test."

"It's a stiff test, mister," answered the tramp, "if you expect me to find that ruby."

John Mordaunt's face looked astounded. An unusual expression for him.

"How the devil—!" he began.

"There's a 'ole in the floor, under the carpet," said the tramp, coolly. "I've 'eard every word."

"That's a very bad beginning!" exclaimed John Mordaunt, with blazing ferocity.

"It seems to me a very good beginning," replied the tramp. "It's orl 'ow you look at it."

John Mordaunt regained his control as suddenly as he had lost it.

"Perhaps you are right," he observed, cool again. "Provided you spy for us instead of against us, it's a useful quality." He took out a cigarette, and slowly lit it. "Then there is no need for explanations between you and me," he said, as he threw the match away. "You know that, from this moment, you are a marked man. You know that you have run up against the secret organization that engineers half the criminal plots in this country. You see, I am not mincing words. You know that Mr Dicks, the genial Norfolk philanthropist, is the mind behind those schemes. You know that the price of betrayal is death."

"That's right," said the tramp. "So your name ain't Dicks?"

"It is not."

"Wot *is* your name, mister?"

"I have a dozen."

"I mean, your *real* name?"

"Apart from myself, that is not known a living soul."

"Wot—not even to Geoffrey Mordaunt, the detective?"

For the second time, astonishment shone in the eye of John Mordaunt. The fingers of his right hand, embedded in his pocket, tightened, and he took a step forward as he stared intently into the tramp's face.

"What made you say that?" he asked.

"Well—'e's supposed to know everything, ain't 'e?" said the tramp. "Besides—"

"Besides—what?"

"'E's your brother."

There was a tense silence. Five seconds ticked by, five seconds that seemed like half a minute to the two men who stood staring at each other in that grim room. John Mordaunt was the first to speak. There was a steely glitter in his eye, a glitter that had made many men quail and whine; but the tramp stood firm, and never lowered his head.

"I think you have about one more minute to live," said John Mordaunt, in a quiet voice. "But, first tell me this. What makes you think that Mordaunt, the detective, is my brother?"

"Because I'm Geoffrey Mordaunt," replied the tramp, as quietly.

The next moment, each man looked down the barrel of a revolver, and each man knew that an instant's wavering might cost him his life. But no shot rang out. The moment was too big for each of them. It was too big for these men who, on a hundred occasions, in their different ways, had crushed all weakness and sentiment out of their beings in the fulfilment of their destinies. The great criminal had it in his power to rid himself of the one brain he feared. The great detective, by the simple pressure of a finger, could destroy the most dangerous criminal schemer of the age. But both men faltered, obeying the strange, unconquerable impulse that divides human beings from machines and alone makes the ceaseless struggle of life bearable.

"It is certain, John, that only one of us will leave this room alive," said Geoffrey, in a voice which he hardly recognized. "Shall we call a temporary truce, and smoke a cigarette?" He was conscious of the fact that both his tone and his words were slightly theatrical, but he was momentarily obsessed by a sense of unreality. Something very real was stirring in his heart, nevertheless. For years he had sought this interview, and, while the world believed that his interest in meeting the master criminal face to face was merely professional, there was a personal reason that had made him desire that meeting passionately. Geoffrey, though he may not have realized it, was an idealist, and, while he worked, he hoped. A shattered ideal did not destroy the ideal to him; it merely spelt human inability to attain it. With a blindness that existed oddly in a man whose vision was otherwise so uncannily clear, he believed that John was not wholly bad, and that his spirit might still be won back to a semblance of what it had once appeared when they played and fought together in the little back-garden of their humble suburban home.

Simultaneously, both men lowered their revolvers. John placed his on a table and Geoffrey followed suit. Then, at John's suggestion, they sat down and faced each other in two chairs out of reach of the table.

"This is folly," said John, "but not unamusing."

He opened his cigarette case, and held it out. "Take one."

"Drugged?" asked Geoffrey.

"Not on this side," replied John.

"Thank you," said Geoffrey, and smiled.

"We cannot talk for long," said John, as he threw his half-smoked cigarette away, and started another. "The others may grow impatient, though I told them to wait until I returned to them. Let our cigarettes determine the length of our chat. When the last of us throws his end away, the truce is over."

"Agreed," answered Geoffrey. He spoke coolly, but a stifling emotion was creeping over him. "John!" he cried, suddenly. "Why are you—as you are?"

"Is this to be a moral lecture?"

"No. A straight talk, between two brothers, one of whom is on his death-bed. In ten minutes, John, you or I will be in the land of the Unknown, and the other will be branded with the sin of Cain!"

John nodded. "Go on," he said, puffing leisurely.

"Thirty years ago," continued Geoffrey, "you and I were small boys together. We used to chat when the lights were out about the future. You remember? It was the same future for both of us, a future filled with wonder and great doings."

"Oh yes, I remember," replied John. "And I remember when our parents separated and ended those chats. You clung to dreams, I learned reality. My father—our father—had his own way of teaching it."

"He was a bad man!"

"And I'm a worse?"

"A hundred times worse, John. But, even so—"

"You think you can change me? Another of your dreams. Listen, Geoffrey. You learned to love the world. I learned to hate it. You can't dream with your eyes open. The world's rotten, rotten to the core, and I'm playing the same game, though in a different way, that is being played by nine hundred and ninety-nine out of every thousand people who appear, in your eyes, respectable. It's the game of Ego. We're all selfish, all for ourselves, and, when we're stripped naked, we see that life is merely a matter of muscle and brain. Morality! There's no such thing! We live by destruction. I take the short cut."

"And does it bring you any happiness?" demanded Geoffrey.

"I don't know what you mean by happiness," retorted John. "I get a certain satisfaction in destroying destroyers—stealing precious jewels that are mockeries, taking wealth from people who have no more right to it than I, killing people quickly who kill other people slowly. I have my passions too." He hesitated for an instant, for Geoffrey's eyes were very like a child's at that moment. "I have learned to hate. I enjoy power. Fools incense me. Sometimes—I fear."

"Are you afraid now?" asked Geoffrey, curiously.

John looked at his cigarette, half-smoked.

"Not in the least," he replied. "I am never afraid when a danger is present. Besides—" He paused. "I know that I shall be the one to leave this room alive."

"You may be right," said Geoffrey, reflectively. "And perhaps it will not make so much difference to the world, after all."

John studied his brother for a second.

"I suppose," he said, slowly, "it would be as hard for me to make you perform a dishonest act as it would be for you to make me perform an honest one?"

"I think so."

"If I let you go—you could not leave me alone?"

"It would be absolutely impossible."

"And it is equally impossible for me to alter my mode of life." He took his cigarette out of his mouth. "Are we wasting time?"

"Very likely. But I want to ask you one more question. That woman—are you fond of her?"

"How can that interest you?"

"As soon as I saw her," said Geoffrey, "I knew her for a cruel, heartless, devilish creature. I know something about her too. Her name is Beatrice Fullerton, and she has caused more than one poor wretch to commit suicide. Have you really fallen so low as that, John?"

"I have no passion of that sort," answered John Mordaunt, "but she is very useful. She would sell her soul for me."

"If she has one," muttered Geoffrey.

"She hasn't," said John, cynically, and threw his cigarette away, though a quarter of it was still unsmoked.

Geoffrey went on puffing. A change began to spread over his features, however. His mouth hardened, as he noted how closely the other was watching his every movement. A minute later, as the cigarette began to burn his lips, he took it out of his mouth.

"And now," observed John Mordaunt, coolly, "I will tell you how I know that I, and not you, will be the one to leave this room alive. I have another revolver in my pocket, and it will be whipped out the moment you throw that cigarette away. I have no need to move from my chair to shoot you dead. It's never been my habit, Geoffrey, to take chances."

Geoffrey frowned, but otherwise showed no emotion.

"I see," he said. "Was it quite cricket?"

"No. It was war."

Geoffrey shrugged his shoulders. After all, was it so unexpected? A great weariness overcame him, a weariness not of the body but of the soul.

"You have a quick brain," continued John, "but I am afraid mine happens to be even quicker. You have given me a chance by which I mean to profit to the fullest extent."

"You can only kill me once."

"True. And the world will think that I have not even done that. I am going to kill you, Geoffrey—you force me to it—but I shall contrive to let the world think that I have been killed, and that you, Geoffrey Mordaunt, are still living. I will step into your shoes. As the great detective, Geoffrey Mordaunt, I shall be able to extend my scope materially. I shall begin, of course, at Littlehampton."

It was a bold scheme, and Geoffrey could not withhold a certain grudging admiration of it. After thinking hard, he again shrugged his shoulders, and, without any logical basis for the dim hope that still glimmered in his breast, prepared to lay down his cigarette-end.

The next moment, he was on his feet. He did not fully realize what had happened, for sometimes, in a great extremity, an idea will flash into one's mind almost simultaneously with action, and the action will be produced without conscious volition. It is as though Time has reversed engines. We have not devised our action; we merely know, afterwards, that we have performed it. Geoffrey was as surprised to find his cigarette-end flying through space as John was. In that, they were equal.

But John suffered the disadvantage of the sudden burning contact, and of the momentary shock of pain it produced. In another moment, Geoffrey had hurled himself after the cigarette-end, and had struck the revolver which John had seized out of his hand.

They were both quick and powerful men. Geoffrey, however, had the advantage of position. Swift as lightning, he secured the revolver himself, and had John covered.

Forced by his adversary, John retreated to the wall. There he stood, in a rage of disappointment. But the fit soon passed. Folding his arms, he smiled defiantly, and waited.

"Shoot," he said. "You've got me."

"God help me!" replied Geoffrey, almost choking with emotion. "I can't shoot my brother in cold blood."

He walked unsteadily to the table, and, picking up his own revolver lying there, handed the other to John.

"If we must fight, let us fight like honourable men," he said, hoarsely. "Take it."

John took the revolver, dazed.

"You've beaten me, Geoff," he whispered. "Quick—before the moment passes!"

And, turning the weapon upon himself, he pressed the trigger.

It was ten minutes before those who clamoured at the door of the chamber of death were admitted. The figure of a tramp lay stretched on the floor, and the figure of John Mordaunt stood over him.

"So you've killed him?" said the beautiful woman. "Well, I daresay it was best."

The figure of John Mordaunt turned towards her, and shuddered. Though his heart ached for the man whose black soul had just entered the next Kingdom, he, too, felt that it was best; and, as he smiled back at the woman who had spoken, his resolve to smash her became as fixed as a frozen star.

CHAPTER 5

Removing his eyes from those of Beatrice Fullerton, Geoffrey Mordaunt stared at the body of his supposed self, lying on the faded carpet, and strove to overcome a great weakness that suddenly swept over him. It was the natural reaction of the past ten minutes, coupled with a dawning realization of the staggering position into which he had placed himself—whether voluntarily or through the strange compulsion of Fate, he could not say.

Geoffrey Mordaunt, to those in the room— to the whole world—lay dead; yet Geoffrey Mordaunt had merely slipped into the body of John, to carry on his work for humanity inside the frame of humanity's arch-enemy. He had reversed the tables upon his brother, borrowing the idea as well as his identity.

For a few moments, as he fought against his weakness, he did not know how he was coming through the ordeal. Emotion battled against wit, in the presence of five pairs of piercing eyes. Every nerve in his body, every thought, every slight action, should be responding to the grim necessity of cheating those eyes, yet the prone figure of his brother, despite all it signified, brought human memories that stirred him deeply. John's last act, he argued, had been a noble one. Surely the God who had silently condemned his life would find some grace in his death. Had Geoffrey followed the natural impulse that moved him, he would have fallen on his knees and prayed for his brother.

How strange, he thought, in a queer, detached way, if this unreasoning love for his brother should prove his own undoing— if the spirit of the dead man, attached still to evil associations, were actually trying to trip him up by a trick of sentiment! Geoffrey did not believe this, but, when once the idea had entered his head, he clung to it tenaciously as a temporary device to stem the emotional tide. He visualized John's spirit laughing at him. It was a child's trick, and he knew it, but it served.

When he raised his eyes again, they were steady and unflinching. There was a hard glitter in them.

"This had to be done," he said, calmly. It was inevitable. You were right in your suspicions, Beatrice."

"Who was he?" she asked.

"You will be surprised when you learn."

"I knew he wasn't a tramp."

Geoffrey nodded. "Your instincts seldom err. Let us go downstairs. I have quite a lot to say."

The tall, thin man interposed with nervous irritation.

"Yes, so have I!" he burst out. "Why didn't you open the door at once?"

Geoffrey looked him full in the face.

"I am beginning to think you need a holiday, my friend," he observed. "This afternoon, you seem to have constituted yourself into a sort of parliamentary Opposition—an Opposition, I may remind you, of one."

There was a laugh, and the tall man flushed; but he repeated his question.

"That's all very well," he grumbled, "but you treat us as though we were children. There's too much mystery. Why were we kept out all this time?"

"For the simple reason," returned Geoffrey Mordaunt, "that I am not able to unlock a door, even to my dearest friend, while a man is sitting on my chest."

"But you called out to us to wait—"

"The man who called out to you was the man on my chest—the tramp—who, since I was quite unable to use my voice myself at that moment, kindly used it for me. He realized, being quite a shrewd fellow, that if he used his own voice you might be less likely to obey the instruction. He quite believed he had me at his mercy, and, I don't mind confessing to you, I cordially agreed with him. But—twenty seconds before you entered —he made the slip that allowed me to reverse the position, and I shot him. You heard the shot. As soon as I had extricated myself, I opened the door."

"There were two shots. Who fired the first one?"

"He did. And missed. After that, we straggled." He paused. "Are you satisfied?"

"Quite, quite," interposed the stout gentleman. "The explanation was unnecessary."

"Yet I recall," proceeded Geoffrey Mordaunt, turning to the last speaker, "that you mistrust everybody, Tobias."

"Perfectly true," beamed the stout gentleman. "So true, in fact, that I sometimes try to soothe the suspicions of those whom I most suspect. If I suspect a person, the very last thing I do is to show it."

He smiled amiably at Geoffrey, who smiled amiably back. It began to dawn upon the detective that the gentleman who went by the name of Tobias might prove one of his stiffest problems.

"But even subtlety must sometimes be leavened with bluntness," said Geoffrey, "and, that being so, I shall count upon you to back me up in a blunt little test which I intend to impose when we go downstairs. If some of us are not treated any worse than children," he added, significantly, with a glance at Edward Tapley, "we may perhaps consider ourselves lucky."

"What the devil do you mean by that?" demanded the tall man.

"I mean," retorted Mordaunt, "that I am by no means convinced we are all friends here, and that I am going to prove or disprove my doubts."

They descended to the lower floor in silence. Once, Mordaunt caught Beatrice's eye fixed upon him quizzically. He smiled slightly in her direction, noting that this vague intimation of a special bond between them satisfied her.

When they reached the room, and seated themselves round the centre table, the silence continued. They were waiting for Mordaunt to speak.

Geoffrey Mordaunt took his time. He knew that this was one

of John's characteristics, and the half-hour which he had spent in the room above, with his ear to the crack in the floor, now proved invaluable. Assisted by his knowledge of their conversation, practised in the art of impersonation, and helped also by the strong physical resemblance between himself and his brother, he felt himself equipped—for the moment, at any rate —to carry out his great deception. He believed that, so far, there was not the shadow of genuine suspicion against him, and he was shrewd enough to attribute the tall man's attitude to jealousy and jangled nerves rather than to suspicion. The attitude, after all, was merely a continuation of the attitude Edward Tapley had shown earlier to John himself.

If he had felt doubts about any of those present, his doubts would have settled first on Tobias.

The company began to fidget, and Geoffrey Mordaunt broke the silence.

"Before I apply my test," he said, looking round searchingly at his companions, "I shall tell you my reasons for it. Incidentally, you are about to learn some startling things. The tramp whose body lies upstairs was not a tramp. He was the cleverest detective of his time—Geoffrey Mordaunt."

It was not unentertaining to the detective to watch their wide-eyed astonishment.

"Geoffrey Mordaunt!" exclaimed Beatrice, while the others stared and gasped.

Mordaunt nodded. "Yes, Geoffrey Mordaunt. And, that being so, perhaps I need not feel too humiliated that he so nearly got by me. He followed me from Norfolk, allaying my suspicions by adopting the attitude of a grateful dog sticking to its master, and by actually putting two other detectives off my track. I recognized the other detectives— both of them. Geoffrey Mordaunt intended, of course, that I should. It gave the tramp the appearance of being definitely on my side. It was a clever trick. I admit, he beat me." He paused. There was admiration in his voice. "In a way, I'm sorry I had to kill him."

"You never did a better bit of work, John," interposed Beatrice sharply.

"I'm inclined to agree with you, my dear. But what will you say when I tell you that I have slain my own brother?"

The astonishment grew.

"This," murmured the stout gentleman, "is getting quite beyond me."

"Do you really mean to say," cried the young man with the scar, "that Geoffrey Mordaunt was your brother? Oh, but that's impossible!"

"Nothing in this world is impossible," replied Mordaunt, blandly. "I think Shakespeare said this before me."

"But why didn't you tell us this?" asked Beatrice.

"I should have thought *your* subtlety would have perceived that. I did not tell you before for the very good reason that Tobias has so eloquently urged this afternoon —namely, that this sad world is so untrusting. It was essential, for all our plans, that you should all of you trust *me*, at any rate. Would your trust have been equal had you known that Geoffrey Mordaunt was my brother?"

"I'm not sure that I should have trusted you less," murmured Tobias.

"I'm sure that *I* should," retorted the tall man, with a sneer. "Why tell us now?"

"Come, come!" remonstrated Mordaunt. "You yourself have complained of mystery. Do not complain now that I remove it! Nevertheless, I assure you I should not have told you that Geoffrey Mordaunt was my brother had I not conclusively proved my sentiments towards him by killing him."

"The evidence," nodded the stout gentleman, "is overwhelmingly in your favour. Overwhelmingly. Did the police know you were brothers?"

"As to that, I cannot say, but I imagine not. It is so long since I shed my original identity. And I think my brother would have been as anxious to disclaim the relationship as I was myself."

Beatrice smiled, and Mordaunt repressed a shudder as he noticed that her smile was positively radiant.

"You have quite a delicious sense of humour, John," she said. "It will be nice when you are able to express it in an atmosphere of respectability."

"That day will come," Mordaunt replied, "when you, Beatrice, are able to smile with the innocence of a little babe."

"Meanwhile," said the tall man, "we wait."

Mordaunt turned his eyes upon him.

"I will satisfy your impatience without further delay," he answered, with a noticeable change in his voice. He spoke sharply now, and decisively. "When my brother thought he had me at his mercy, he told me certain things. Some of these things were true, and some, possibly, lies. He convinced me of one thing. Our position is more rocky than I had supposed, and the net is being drawn around us. This will mean an entire reorganization of our plans and meeting-places. We shall certainly avoid this house in future, for instance. I will have to work out a fresh programme, for Geoffrey Mordaunt's death, when it becomes known, will rouse Scotland Yard as nothing else has roused it. It's a blow right at their heart—in the dead centre of their vanity. Well, we'll have to act accordingly. I already have certain plans in my head, which we will discuss later. But at the moment I am more concerned with other information he gave me." He paused. "it was to the effect that we had a traitor among us. A traitor—in this very house."

There was a silence. Beatrice broke it by asking, coolly:

"And did you believe him?"

"I'm not sure. Anyway, it will be quite simple to prove."

"And how do you propose to prove it?"

"Oh, but this is ridiculous!" cried the young man with the scar. "We've worked together too long to believe any such story."

"Is that Tobias's view?" asked Mordaunt.

"What's he mean by traitor?" asked the dwarf.

"He said very clearly what he meant. He said that someone here was an impersonator."

"And what's *that* mean?" asked the dwarf again.

"One man pretending to be another."

"Oh, then I'm all right," said the dwarf. "No one'd pretend they was me. No one'd want to. I'm Joe, all right. P'raps one day I'll wish I wasn't.'"

"I hope one day you will, my friend—and I think it will not be long in coming," thought Mordaunt, as the unpleasant creature grinned and spat.

"This is going too far altogether," exclaimed the tall man, fiercely. "Personally, I refuse to submit to any test! I may tell you —John—that my section are none too happy about you lately. There may be trouble one day."

"Well, I wouldn't anticipate the day," replied Mordaunt, smoothly, "by making an enemy of a man whose help you never needed more than you do at this moment. I hold the key to the whole situation. Without me, you'll come down like a house of cards. Without me, you'll never trace that ruby, Joe will swing, Tobias's scheme for stirring up the unemployed will never come off, and your own dissatisfied section will turn and rend the thing that is nearest to them. You need me. You know it. And, that being so, I mean to run the show in my own fashion, and to clear away every single doubt as soon as it appears."

"I protest! I won't submit to it!" cried the objector.

"Say the word, guv'nor," said the dwarf, looking at Mordaunt, and with his hand in his hip-pocket.

"Put that back!" commanded Mordaunt, in a stern voice. "If we'd reached that point, I have no doubt Mr Tapley could be quite as ready with his revolver as you with yours. Besides I am sure he will not object to the test, when he hears it. There is nothing degrading about it. It is simply this: I want a short account, from each of you, of your doings during the last three days. Beatrice, please find some paper, and let everyone have a sheet. Each account will end with the full name of the writer and his present address. The papers shall, of course, be destroyed here, on the spot, as soon as I have satisfied myself that they are correct."

"What about me?" asked the dwarf. "I ain't much good at writing."

"You can draw pictures in the sand."

"Yes. But—"

"I know what you're thinking, Joe. You're thinking that your own account won't make very pretty reading. Well, rest assured. Not one paper shall ever leave this room, saving in the form of ashes."

"I think the idea is quite a reasonable one," said Tobias, smiling whimsically. "Unfortunately, I've had rather a dull time during the past three days, but I'll do the best I can." He took the sheet of paper which Beatrice held out to him. "Yes, an excellent idea. You, of course, will join us in our little game?"

The question was addressed to Mordaunt.

"Certainly," he replied promptly. "You will not find Mr Dicks in the least reticent."

He could not repress a secret smile. Having watched his brother religiously for three days, he knew that his job would be a simple one. The only trouble that faced him was the question of his handwriting.

"I bow to the majority," said the tall man, "but—understand—I protest."

For fifteen minutes, pencils ran over paper in that strange room, while the sun sank behind a bank of clouds and hastened the gathering gloom. Mordaunt, writing rapidly, was the first to finish. Having done so, he carefully folded his paper over, and then leaned back in his chair, waiting. As he watched his five companions scribbling details which would have interested him sufficiently before he assumed his present role, but which were even more important to him now, the sense of unreality which had pervaded him many times that afternoon returned to him with renewed force. Were these, indeed, real people? They appeared to him more like children playing a game round a table! Was he himself real? Was not the whole thing some absurd, fantastic dream?

Then the irony of the situation came over him. Five criminals making confessions for the protection of the enemy in their midst! Had any one of them known that Mordaunt's sole reason for requiring these accounts lay in his necessity for learning facts, not for checking them, his life would not have been worth a second's purchase.

He controlled a sudden desire to laugh. Humorous though the situation might appear, it was tragic enough in its portent. Each "child," playing that round game, was a sinner of the first water, and there never was a sinner who failed to offer, on occasions, food for laughter, or even for some softer emotion; but the rarity of these occasions, and the accidental nature of their origin, render them unimportant to all save the psychologist and the sentimentalist, and Geoffrey Mordaunt was a man of facts, despite his dreams. He saw the humour, the ironic pathos of the situation, but he was not in his heart amused by it.

Presently, the pencils stopped writing, one by one, and the papers, by his order, were handed to him. When he had collected them all, he took up his own folded sheet, and, striking a match, set light to it.

"Are we not to see?" asked Tobias, mildly.

"I wrote to satisfy you," replied Mordaunt, "but, as I can repeat what I have written word for word, there is no need to trouble you with the document. It will save time if I tell you my story, without putting each of you to the necessity of reading it.

He gave his account, clearly and concisely, while his tell-tale writing shrivelled into ashes. His audience listened closely and made no comment. Then he took up the first of his companions' sheets. It was signed "Joe Flipp," and was a sheet for which the Public Prosecutor would have given very considerably at that moment. But, true to his promise—and much against his secret will—Mordaunt set light to it after he had read it out to the company.

The next paper was that written by the tall, thin man. His name, the paper corroborated, was Edward Tapley, and Geoffrey committed the name, together with many other interesting particulars, to his memory. Third was the confession of Tobias King. Tobias's document contained many details, of varying importance. He described minutely the doses of medicines he took, and how, on one occasion, he had forgotten to take a dose altogether. These details annoyed Edward Tapley, but they interested the man who read them out, for he could not afford to miss any material that supplied a key to the psychology of his companions. Their psychology was as important as their actions. Tobias King might have been a real humorist had he been born in wedlock, of a mother who had not been addicted to drugs, and of a father who had not escaped life imprisonment by taking poison.

"All correct?" asked Tobias.

"Perfectly," replied Mordaunt, studying him.

"I'm sorry to disappoint you," said Tobias, "but there was one distinct lie in it."

"Unless you are referring to one of your allusions to physic," observed Mordaunt, evenly, "the only lie of which I can accuse you is the one now on your lips."

"Quite right, quite right," murmured Tobias. "I really think I shall have to trust you, after all."

"I really think you will," said Mordaunt, but his heart was beating a little faster than usual. If Tobias King had been a trifle less subtle, and had really inserted a lie, it might have spelt the end.

The fourth paper was signed "Arthur Lancing, *alias* George Finch, *alias* Alf. Smith." The fifth and last was Beatrice Fullerton's. Geoffrey Mordaunt read this through with particular care, noting the feminine touches as well as the facts, the glimpses of character that lurked in every sentence, the fine, firm writing. Then he struck a match, and, lighting a comer of the paper, watched the flame burn words which his mind retained.

Never before had a detective obtained such evidence, and as speedily destroyed it!

"And now I hope you're satisfied," said Edward Tapley, when the paper was reduced to ashes.

"Absolutely satisfied," replied Geoffrey Mordaunt. "I am satisfied that my brother, in his endeavour to render my last moments uncomfortable, went beyond the truth. This was, perhaps, consistent, showing that he overreached himself in speech as well as in action. It marked his one weakness, his one flaw. But perhaps, after all, he achieved some object, for he has made us waste some very valuable time. Come, let us now bend our thoughts on Littlehampton."

They sat there for an hour, discussing plans and projects, while the day died outside and the shadows grew around them. They lit no light. The gloom suited their moods. As flowers turn towards the sun, so dark thoughts blossom best in darkness. And, while they chatted in low voices, the spirit that should have been with them had slipped from its earthly husk upstairs to meet its new experiences, and little ragged street urchins bawled out their news.

CHAPTER 6

A ragged, undersized man stood on the beach of Littlehampton, cap in hand, beside a sand-picture of a lighthouse. There was a certain stiff neatness about the picture, but the lighthouse was as out of proportion as was the little man himself, and leered as grotesquely at the world. If diseases can be drawn in the sand, that lighthouse was pathological, a mute reflection of the mind that had created it.

But holiday crowds are not apt to be critical, a fact to which the state of the sand-artist's hat bore testimony. It was well lined with coppers, and—so perverse are the workings of pathology—the thicker that copper lining grew the more dejected became the face of the sand-artist. Like a woman who successfully sheds tears to get a hat, and then sheds more tears to get a gown, the sand-artist grew sadder and sadder as his need for sadness grew less.

But, suddenly, he forgot for a moment to be sad. A new expression leapt into his eye. It was only, however, for an instant; he relapsed into his dejection almost immediately afterwards, and jerked his hat in the direction of two new-comers who had just joined the crowd.

"Give him a penny," said the woman of the couple—a slim, girlish woman, whose lines were gracefully reflected in her grey dress, and whose rich auburn hair escaped in little clusters beneath her close-fitting hat.

"No, I don't believe in indiscriminate charity," replied the man. "He ought to get some useful work to do,"

"But the poor fellow's a dwarf!" exclaimed the woman. "What useful work *could* he do?"

She listened for his reply with secret amusement.

"It might be good work if he stopped drawing bad light-houses," said the man. She shot a glance at him, and some instinct impelled him to add, "Still, even a dwarf who draws bad lighthouses may have his uses, eh?"

"Ah," she observed cryptically, as they turned to go.

They directed their steps across the sandy common towards a cheerful, ruddy house which, though little different from its neighbours, held a special interest for them, and also, apparently, for a young man in regulation holiday attire—white trousers, grey flannel jacket, straw hat, and a tie rather too brilliant—who stood outside, staring up at it. Like dozens of other houses in the row, it bore the inscription "Apartments," fearing that the world would pass it by in ignorance of an obvious fact. The season was not far advanced, but many of the houses were occupied by visitors, as was evidenced by towels and bathing-dresses hung out of windows to dry.

The young man made no movement to depart as the couple approached. He seemed rather pleased to see them, and, when they paused, he addressed them as though possessing the right of a common interest.

"This is the house—No. 22," said the young man.

"I beg your pardon?" replied the bearded gentleman.

He spoke with a slight foreign accent. They looked, indeed, like a couple from the Continent.

"I say, this is the house," repeated the young man, blinking amiably. "Queer affair, wasn't it?"

"I'm afraid I don't understand," said the bearded one.

The young man whistled. "What, you don't mean to tell me —? Well, I'm dashed! The papers are full of it. It's the house where that man lived—the one who was chased on the evening James Smith was murdered. You've heard about that, of course?"

The bearded man shook his head, while his pretty companion explained.

"We have only recently come from the Continent, and have

hardly looked at the papers yet. Who was this James Smith?"

"Did I say James Smith?" exclaimed the young man, ingenuously. "I meant James Cardhew, of course. He was murdered about three miles from here, in a lonely house, and that same evening they suspected a fellow named Smith—that's how I got the names mixed—who was living in this house. They went to arrest him, but he jumped out of the window—that's the one, on the first floor— heaven knows how he managed it—and led them the deuce of a chase. In the end, they shot him."

The speaker's eyes glowed with all the enthusiasm of that strange mixture of innocence and morbidness which causes so many people to waste pennies on afternoon papers. He stared at the couple, as though anxious to see their eyes start out of their heads. His information, however, was received coolly.

"Perhaps this kind of thing doesn't interest you," said the young man, rather lamely. "But I thought it might, as I saw you staring at the house. I admit, I can hardly tear myself away."

"We paused because we were looking for rooms," answered the bearded man, "and, as a matter of fact, your story interests me very much indeed. I happen to be writing a book on criminology." He glanced enquiringly at his companion. "A chat with the landlady ought to be worth while. What do you think?"

"Quite a good idea," she replied. "We might even take the room. It would give you a good 'atmosphere' for your work."

"Ah, but you won't be able to," interposed the young man. "They're occupied by two young ladies who came down the day after the murder. What do you think of that? Rather plucky, what?"

"Yes, quite plucky," said the woman. "Although, after all, what is there to be afraid of now?"

"Well, I don't know," exclaimed the young man. "A valuable ruby was stolen, and it's never turned up yet. The police have searched the room and can't find a trace of it. But you never know, do you? It might be there still, hidden away somewhere, and they might come back for it." He stared, fascinated, up at the window, "You never know, do you?"

"Well, we'll interview the landlady, anyhow," said the man with the beard, with a note of finality in his voice. "We're very much obliged to you for your information."

"Not at all, not at all," answered the young man, and raised his hat politely as they ascended the broad white steps to the front door. He watched them ring the bell, and then, as though realizing that curiosity can be carried too far, he turned abruptly on his heel and strolled away towards the sea, with his hands stuck resolutely in his pockets. But he could not refrain from looking back once or twice, as he crossed the grassy common leading to the sands, and he noted that the conversation on the door-step was rather a long one.

Holiday idlers are notoriously curious, but this young man seemed to be particularly so. He appeared, in fact, to be made up of curiosity. The warm afternoon sunshine, beating down upon him while he sat on a seat, ought to have made him drowsy, but, instead of yielding to the temptations of sleep or of indolent semi-alertness, he stared, often open-mouthed, at nearly everyone who passed him. One girl, incensed by what she considered an excess of temerity, gave him a scornful look. She was, however, mistaken. He had not been staring at her at all, but at two figures in the distance, across the common, disappearing into a house.

"Upon my word," thought the young man, "those people seem as interested in that house as I am myself."

He rose, and went on to the sands. The dwarf was still doing good business. He walked up to the depressing work of art, now slightly defaced by careless feet, and wondered whether any standard was imposed on sand-artists. He decided that it was not. From the look of the dwarf's hat, none appeared necessary.

"Doin' good trade?" he said, to the sand-artist.

"Look's more'n it is," replied the dwarf, miserably. "It don't go fur when you 'as to keep an old mother and a dyin' sister."

"Well, it doesn't seem to me you're doing so badly," observed the other. "How do you work this? Do you stay in one place all the summer?"

"No, I moves along," answered the dwarf.

"I see. And when's your time up here?"

"Don't know, sir. Move when I feel like it. Might be to-morrer. Might be nex' week. Can't say."

"Well, here's another penny, and good luck," said the young man.

A quarter of an hour later, as he strolled once more across the lawn, he saw the couple he had spoken to leave No. 22 Marine Row. He was dawdling after them when a girl came out of the house. This seemed to undecide him, but, after the briefest hesitation, he went up to the girl, and lifted his hat.

She looked surprised, and a faint flush spread over her cheek.

"I hope you'll forgive me," he said, "but my name's Wilfred Hobson, and I want you to know that, if ever you're in any difficulty, or want help or advice, you can count on me."

Then he took off his hat again, and left her. She looked after him in profound astonishment, wondering why she were not feeling more annoyed.

"Of all the cool young men!" she thought. "Why should I be in any difficulty? And why should he want to help me, if I am?"

Nevertheless, a tiny, intangible load had been lifted from her heart.

Meanwhile, Wilfred Hobson was wandering with apparent aimlessness in the track of the couple, whom he had no difficulty in keeping in sight. He saw them turn into an hotel, and his heart purred with pleasure that they should have selected the very hotel he was staying in himself. This was not very surprising, perhaps, because it happened to be the best hotel in the town.

Wilfred Hobson dawdled on. He was in no hurry. He lit a cigarette, and stopped to watch a child riding a donkey, and a kite soar high up into the sky. Then he ambled on again, and entered the hotel at four o'clock.

"Are you taking tea, sir?" asked the head waiter, meeting him in the hall.

"Yes, please," yawned the young man.

"I'm afraid your usual table is occupied," said the waiter, "but I'll send your tea to the table next to it."

"All the same to me, so long as it's got a sea view," replied Wilfred Hobson, as he entered the luxurious chamber in which tea was served. "A sea view's nothing to you, but it would be if you lived in London."

The waiter smiled, and ushered him to his table. At the next table sat the foreign-looking couple.

Hobson glanced at them in pleasurable surprise, and nodded to them as he sat down. His appearance seemed to have interrupted the flow of their conversation, but he showed, in an obvious manner, that he did not want to intrude, and, while waiting for his tea, he propped a weekly humorous journal up against a flower vase, and buried himself in it. Evidently the jokes amused him, for his face beamed, and, every now and again, he laughed. When the waiter appeared with his tray, he was poring over a picture.

"Do you speak French?" he asked the waiter.

"No, sir," answered the waiter.

"Well, I wish you did! There's a joke here with a French word in it, and blessed if I can understand it."

"Perhaps I can help you?" said the gentleman at the next table, bending forward.

"I wish you would, sir," replied Hobson. "There—what's that mean?"

"That's French for 'pig,'" explained the gentleman, examining the paper. "The Englishman has called the driver a pig instead of a coachman. The words are very similar."

"Ha, ha! Damn good!" laughed Hobson. "Thanks awfully." And he buried himself once more.

Conversation flowed again between the couple at the next table. Now, they spoke in French. For a man who had just confessed that he did not understand French, Hobson's ears were curiously alert. He did not learn much, however, and he attributed the fact to the superior strategy of the woman.

"What devils some women are," he thought, as he stared hard

at a comic picture. "And how they twist men! I believe that woman could inspire a man to write an ode or commit a murder."

Presently the gentleman rose, observing that he would go and see about the luggage.

"I don't suppose you want to come?" he asked his companion. They had relapsed now into English.

"No, thanks," she answered. "I think I'll stay here for ten minutes and smoke a cigarette."

The gentleman went out, and the lady leisurely extracted a small cigarette-case from her bag. She put a cigarette between her lips, then sought for matches, and found none. Hobson dived in, with all the impetuosity of youth.

"I've got a light," he exclaimed, and held it out to her. "Good God," he thought, as the match glowed on her face, and she thanked him with her eyes. "I don't wonder some men make fools of themselves!"

"Did your friend get any stuff for his book out of the landlady?" he asked, as he blew the match out.

"Oh yes," replied the woman. "She was most voluble." She smiled at him. There was a quality in the smile that made Wilfred Hobson immediately alert, but his face did not show it.

"There was no chance of getting rooms there, of course?" he said.

"None at all. Personally, I'm glad. I hate criminology. I like this much better." She looked at him, shading her eyes with her lashes. "Why is it," she asked, abruptly, "that English people are so—so aloof?"

"Are we?" he blinked.

"Yes, terribly. On the Continent, it is so different. Do you know, you're the first Englishman who has ever made me feel at home without a formal introduction."

"No! Really? Ah, but you haven't been here long, you know," he reminded her.

"This isn't my first visit."

There was an awkward little pause. What was she driving at?

The truth suddenly dawned upon Wilfred Hobson, but he received his inspiration a moment too late. She was saying:

"I'm going to ask you a very great favour —you make me feel I can. Will you give me some advice about some English papers I've got to fill in? I don't understand them."

"Why, of course," he replied.

"Thank you so much. It is most confusing, being a foreigner. After I've finished this cigarette, I'll go and get them. They are in my bag."

"Now, I wonder," thought Hobson, "why she is trying to keep me here?"

She smoked slowly, chatting all the while. Then, at last, she rose, and said she would find the papers. She was gone five minutes, and returned with a tragic face.

"What do you suppose?" she exclaimed. "I cannot find my bag. It must be at the station. You are so wonderfully kind that I hate to worry you further—but *would* you come to the station with me? These officials confuse me. We'll drive there—it won't take long. Perhaps we'll meet my husband. If not, I know he'll be as grateful to you as I for helping me."

Hobson thought for a moment. If his suspicions were unfounded, there could be no harm in complying with this request. On the other hand, if he was right in his conjecture that these two people were crooks, it was all the more important for him to act the innocent. He decided to accompany her to the station, thereby maintaining his character as an easygoing holiday simpleton. If the bag were not there, he would be strengthened in his conclusions, and break away from her at the earliest opportunity. For it would then be obvious, he argued, that she was deliberately trying to keep him away from her husband—if, indeed, the man with the beard were her husband— and that it was up to him to discover what this man was doing.

They went to the station. The bag was not found. Saying that he had an appointment with his hairdresser, Hobson put his companion into a trap, and directed the driver to take her back to the hotel.

It was merely to give the appearance of veracity to his excuse that he dived into a hairdresser's and had a hasty shave. Immediately afterwards, he dived out again, and spent a profitable hour at his favourite occupation of lounging on the front. He noted four things, and each one was associated with the foreign-looking man with the beard; for, to his relief, he had little difficulty in picking him up.

The first was that this man had a long conversation with the diminutive sand-artist, by a breakwater some little way from the town. The dwarf appeared to be receiving instructions, and, at one moment, there was a slight altercation, the dwarf giving way at the end with a bad grace, dominated by a greater personality. The second thing Hobson noticed was that another conversation took place between his quarry and a boatman. The boatman's face was a study, and he, too, seemed to remonstrate mildly at one stage. But again, the greater personality won. Evidently, the bearded gentleman was a master at his trade.

The third item was another conversation, this time between the bearded gentleman and the pretty girl who lived at No. 22 Marine Row. This conversation was the one that puzzled Wilfred Hobson most. The girl looked annoyed and distressed, and, once, he caught a look of distress on the face of the bearded gentleman. Real distress, it seemed to Hobson, not the emulated article. Quite different from the emulated distress, for instance, with which the gentleman concluded the interview, and walked slowly off.

It was while watching this departure that Hobson made his fourth discovery. He discovered that he had met the man before, but he could not for the life of him say when or where. Something about him, however, was vaguely familiar. He was convinced that this was not their first meeting or encounter.

It had been said by those at Scotland Yard who were jealous of Mr Hobson's progress, and of the interest shown in him by Geoffrey Mordaunt, the greatest among them, that he was slow to make up his mind. Perhaps he did err slightly on the side of caution, failing fully to realize that one has occasionally to risk one's reputation for accuracy in order to save a second in time and a man's life. But not even his worst enemy could say that, once his mind was made up, it wavered. Behind his ingenuous blue eyes there was a spirit of indomitable determination which argued well for his future, though it may not have spelt a green old age to the prophets. Determination needs to be leavened with luck if it is to progress unscathed. When luck is set dead against it, it merely differs from the lesser qualities in the method of its death. It does not linger, but smashes itself into a brick wall.

Wilfred Hobson was hesitating now. He was wondering whether the moment were ripe to play some definite cards he possessed. For ten minutes he had noted how earnestly the tall, bearded gentleman staying at the hotel had conversed with the wonderfully charming girl who was staying at No. 22 Marine Row. He noted the reluctance with which he left her, and the relief with which she watched him go.

"Damn shame," thought Wilfred Hobson. "Why can't they leave girls out of it?"

His mind was made up. Time for action had arrived. Precisely what action he did not know, but he meant to find out. He walked straight up to the girl, and raised his hat.

"If the mountain won't come to Mohammed, Mohammed must go to the mountain," he said. "Can I help you, Miss Heather?"

He spoke in a natural, matter-of-fact voice. The vapidness of an idle holiday-maker had entirely departed.

Joan Heather looked at him for a moment before replying. It was not her custom to accept the advances of strange men—either with beards or without—but she felt the genuineness of her present companion's attitude, and she was, indeed, in a mood of doubt. The girl-friend who had come to Littlehampton with her had been suddenly recalled to town, and she was utterly alone.

"How do you know my name?" she asked. "I ought to be surprised, but, somehow, I'm not."

"I know a good many things," replied Wilfred Hobson, "and I hope—for both our sakes—that you are going to help me to know some more."

"What other things do you know?"

"I know that the gentleman who has just left you seems fonder of you than you do of him, and that you are troubled about him."

"Do you know *his* name?"

Hobson shook his head.

"There you beat me. I don't. I haven't the least idea. But I know it isn't the name he has given you,"

"And how do you know that?"

"Because he is concealing his real identity."

"Well, he admitted that he was," said Joan Heather, "the first time I saw him."

"When he called with his lady friend at your house?"

"Yes. Is there anything you don't know?"

"Too much, unfortunately. Why did he say he was hiding his identity?"

"He is a writer on crime, and is travelling incognito."

"Bah!" exclaimed Wilfred Hobson. "Writers on crime don't travel incognito. They're too jolly proud of their reputations. Would you mind telling me some other things he said?"

"Certainly. They wanted to see the rooms—like dozens of others who have called. These visitors are a positive nuisance, Mr Hobson."

"Ah, you've remembered my name, I see. That's a good mark for you—and for me. Did he try to take the rooms?"

"Yes. The lady seemed particularly anxious—"

"And she told me she hated criminology!" murmured the young man.

"They almost tried to frighten me away, saying that someone might come back, one night for the ruby that was never discovered. Do you think they will?"

"I shouldn't be at all surprised. Miss Heather," replied Wilfred Hobson, slowly, "and that's just why I'm here, at this moment. I don't trust that bearded man one little bit."

"Don't you believe he's really a writer on criminology, then?"

"No—but I'll wager he knows the subject, Though! I'll wager he's steeped in it. I'll tell you something else I know. He's thick with the dwarf who draws pictures in the sand—a devil in rags, if there ever was one. One thing that beats me is his carelessness in not spotting me when I've been watching him. That's a puzzle —though I admit I've not played my part so badly, and may have hoodwinked him. Not so his wife, though. She kept me at her heels for half an hour, as though she knew I was simply itching to stalk her husband."

"Now, please, tell me something," said Joan. "Why should you itch to stalk her husband?"

"Because I'm a detective."

Joan smiled, and there was relief in her smile.

"I think I guessed you were," she responded. "You see, whenever you've been about, I've felt secure."

"I'm not sure that that's a compliment to my disguise," laughed Wilfred Hobson, "but I'll take it as a personal compliment, anyway. What made you think I was a detective?"

"I can't say. A sixth sense, perhaps. No, but it became more than that, after you spoke to me outside my house this afternoon. I thought I recognized your name. I believe my fiancé once mentioned it. I am engaged to Geoffrey Mordaunt."

Hobson held out his hand immediately.

"Really?" he exclaimed. "I congratulate you both on your luck. You're going to marry one of the best, Miss Heather, and I only wish Mordaunt were here to help me with my present little tangle. But he's on another job—rather a mysterious one, and it's taking him rather longer than I expected. Perhaps you know something about it?"

"I know nothing," she answered. "I never ask questions, and he is never very communicative on the subject of his work."

"Of course not. I might have guessed that. Old Mordaunt is a frightfully conscientious chap, and I hope you'll never put it down to cooling affection, or anything of that sort, if he doesn't tell you certain things after you're married. It's wonderful how things leak out in this game. One can't be too tight. And then, too, knowledge is sometimes dangerous."

A shadow passed across Joan's face.

"I know that quite well," she answered, in a voice that trembled a little. "It worries me sometimes. Geoffrey must have piles of enemies. And it's a week since I had any news of him."

"Don't worry. Miss Heather," answered Hobson, reassuringly, hiding the fact that he was hardly less worried himself than she was. "Mordaunt knows how to look after himself. Detectives have to disappear sometimes for a day or two. Well, let's get back to business. Our bearded friend could not frighten you out of your rooms. So then he tried some other method. I take it that he was trying while he was talking to you just now—and that he failed. What did he want?"

"What do you think? He wanted to take me out for a row this evening!"

Hobson almost laughed. "Well, I must say, he doesn't look much like a holiday butterfly! It's quite clear, Miss Heather, that he has some special reason for wanting you out of the place this evening."

"But the row was only to be for an hour—from eight to nine,"

"Long enough for a search, perhaps. But it's an odd hour to choose. By Jove, I've an idea! Wait for me here. Miss Heather, will you? There's that fisherman chap over there." I want to speak to him."

He strode across, and accosted the fisherman, who was smoking by his boat.

"I want you to take me out for a row this evening," said Hobson. "Can you manage eight o'clock?"

"I ain't sure, sir," replied the fisherman, frowning. "I think I've fixed up for that time with another gent."

"Oh, that's a pity. What time will you be back?"

"Oh—nine or ten, I suppose." The man spoke uneasily.

"Make it nine. I'll book you for that hour."

"I tell you, I don't know what time I'll be back, sir," exclaimed the fisherman, crossly. "I ain't taking any more orders."

"Not even if I were to offer you a pound, eh?"

The fisherman took his pipe out of his mouth, and stared at Hobson.

"What's the game, sir?" he demanded.

"That's exactly what I'm going to find out," retorted Hobson. "I offer you a pound to take me out for an hour, and you hesitate. I want to know why? Has someone offered you more?"

"Here, I'm not going to answer any more questions—"

"It's the only way," answered Hobson, coolly, "to avoid being marched straight off to the police station. My name is Hobson. I'm a detective. At the moment, I'm your friend, because I happen to be after bigger fry than you. But, unless you tell me the exact arrangement you entered into with the gentleman with the beard within sixty seconds, I'll put the law into motion against you. I know a trifle more than you think, my friend."

The fisherman gave up.

"I was to take his party out, and then act as if the tide was carrying us off. I was to pretend I couldn't get back till two o'clock. I thought it was only some silly joke, sir, and that's God's truth—"

"You've told me all I want to know," interrupted Hobson, sternly. "You've acted like a fool, and can be thankful I've no time to waste on prize idiots. That trip won't come off. Either it will be cancelled, or you'll not see the gentleman again. Now, listen to me, and think well over my words. Are you attending?"

"Yes, sir—yes, sir!" mumbled the fisherman, growing terrified.

"At any moment, I can give information which will clap you into prison. If you breathe one single word of your conversation with me to a living soul, to prison you'll go. I'm taking the view that, in associating with a crook, you've only been a fool. But others might take a more serious view. Do you get me?"

"Yes, sir," answered the fisherman, thoroughly awed.

Turning on his heel, Hobson retraced his steps, and Joan rose from her seat to meet him.

"Let's stroll," said Hobson. "It will attract less attention. My worst fears are justified, Miss Heather." And he told her his news.

"What do you make of it?" asked Joan, bewildered.

"It's as easy as two and two," replied Hobson. "That man is connected with the murder case, and he knows where the ruby is. Well, by George, I'll chalk him up a good mark if he can show me where, for I've ransacked that room from top to bottom, and had come to the conclusion that it was a wash-out."

"When did you ransack my room, Mr Hobson?" she asked.

"Oh, one time," he grinned. "There's not much a burglar can teach a detective. He thought hard. "This is a delicate job, Miss Heather. We've got to secure our quarry, but we've also got to avoid scaring them. Don't you see, if we simply collar them as they enter, we shall be no wiser than we are now about that ruby. Evidently, it's going to take some little time to get, for they want a perfectly clear field, and plenty of time. Yes, they must show us where the ruby is first, and then we'll hand them the cuffs." He paused, and looked at her quizzically. She marvelled to see the keenness in his eye and to feel the clear intelligence of his mind, which contrasted so oddly with the vacuous, good-natured youth of his previous role. "I wonder," he said, slowly, "if you oughtn't to go on that boat trip, after all?"

"You mean that, if I don't, they may not risk the raid?"

"That's just what I do mean. It's a pretty point. Wait a minute. Let's think." His mind worked rapidly. "No," he said, at last, "I'm inclined to think we'd better let matters rest. If you suddenly change your mind, it will look suspicious. They may get the wind up. No, they'll visit the place, anyway. Probably they mean to flit tonight, and the hotel won't find them in the morning. They've brought no luggage. Yes, it's to be a quick job—and, if necessary, a desperate one."

"There's one thing you've forgotten," said Joan. "If I'd taken that boat trip—"

"He'd have been away too. That's true. But I expect he'd have fixed that somehow, and, even if he were not present himself, there's the woman, and the sand-artist— I'll wager he's in it, up to the neck—and heaven knows how many more lurking round corners."

"And the fisherman?"

"No, he's just a fool. By Jove, Miss Heather!" he exclaimed, as the idea grew in his mind, "this is going to be a big thing, and I'm not going to leave anything to chance. We'll have plenty of men on the job, and, with your permission, we'll commandeer your premises for the evening. You and your landlady had better lock yourselves up in a room in the basement. There may be some liveliness!"

"Shall we go next door?" suggested Joan.

"In one way, I'd like it. But, if they got wind of it, the whole show would be given away. That would never do. No, lock yourself up in some room in the basement, and you'll be safe. I'll see there's a police officer to look after you. And, now, I must be off. Believe me," he added chuckling, "in five minutes, there'll be some buzz at the local police station, and I shall be a little tin god!"

"Look after yourself, Mr Hobson," she said, as they shook hands. "I should be very unhappy if anything happened to you."

"Don't worry—I'm not one to put my head into the lion's mouth," he lied. "There's only one thing I regret. I wish Geoffrey Mordaunt were here. He ought to be, because, if a certain theory of mine is right, this is going to be the biggest scoop we've ever had. I've got ideas about that bearded fellow. If he's the chap I'm beginning to take him For, Miss Heather, I'm about to land the fish that Mordaunt has been trying to land for the last ten years!"

"Who's that?" she asked.

"The cleverest and most devilish criminal," he replied, "that the world has ever known."

CHAPTER 7

Geoffrey Mordaunt's spirit should have been buoyant as he returned to his hotel, where Beatrice Fullerton awaited him. All his plans had run smoothly. All the seeds he had sown had blossomed, he felt sure, in the fertile brain of Hobson. There would be some splendid captures before the next sunrise, and the trap into which he and his accomplices were about to walk was so complete that he wondered how he himself would be able to wriggle out of it—and to wriggle out of it he was fully determined. His mission was to allow others to be caught, not himself.

But there was very little joy in Geoffrey's soul. Abhorring criminality with an honest hatred, and straining every nerve and muscle to defeat its ends, he felt nevertheless as though he had, even in these few short hours, absorbed some of its poison into his system, as though he were becoming an entity quite separate from the world of respectability in which he had always moved—in mufti, at any rate; and the unpleasant role in which he had just been forced to appear before his own fiancée was not the least of his present burdens. He now saw the wretched fascination of crime from the inside, he was discovering the subtle psychology of it, the strange excuses for it, the centre of the sphere in which he dwelt. Beatrice, cold and cruel, was none the less beautiful on that account, and was none the less able to incite the eternal response in a man. If anything, Geoffrey Mordaunt hated Beatrice Fullerton now more than he had ever hated her before—because now, in his own person, he understood the devilish discords she could sow in one's soul.

"Well?" she greeted him. "Is everything arranged?"

"Everything," he replied.

"Tell me your plans," she said.

"My plans are very simple. Everything, barring a few details, has worked out as I had hoped. The only person I am really anxious about is Edward Tapley."

"What's wrong with him?"

"Well, he's losing his nerve—and he's got to climb across three roofs."

"He can climb like a cat!"

"I know he can. But he's been drinking. You remember how troublesome he was at our last meeting, Beatrice?"

She nodded.

"And yet," said Geoffrey Mordaunt, swiftly, "you wanted me to trust him with the place where the ruby is hidden? Tobias was quite right when he said we could trust nobody."

"Don't you trust even me?"

He smiled back into her eyes. She had drawn closer to him, and seemed to be piercing his soul.

"I trust you," answered Geoffrey, "as I would trust John Mordaunt himself."

"Is that the truth, John?"

"The absolute truth, Beatrice."

"You are a strange man, John. You are the only man whose heart I can never wholly read. What is your secret?"

"My secret?"

"Yes, your secret!" she exclaimed, half-petulantly. "How is it that you can resist what no other man can resist?"

"Meaning yourself?" he asked, coolly.

"Meaning myself."

"Perhaps I realize that the sweet loses its power as soon as it is tasted. Perhaps I appreciate you so much, Beatrice, that I do not want to spoil you. Would your interest in me be as great if you had probed what you call my secret?"

"I don't know," she confessed.

"Well, I do know. You have probed the secrets of many men, and have thrown them aside afterwards. How would you feel if

I did the same with you? I am protecting you by refusing your embraces."

He spoke half-banteringly, but she felt the keen edge of his words.

"I detest you!" she fired back. "How can you compare us with fools?" Suddenly she put her lips close to his. "Do you think, if you kissed me, that you *could* throw me aside?" She drew her face away again sharply. "But you shall not kiss me! One day you will melt. Meanwhile, let us get back to business."

"That will suit me admirably."

"You've seen Tapley?"

"That was my first business on leaving you. He is to let us in at one o'clock by the back door. Joe and I will be waiting in the garden. We ought to be through with it by half-past, but it may take longer. You will be waiting with the car at the spot arranged."

"Suppose the ruby isn't there, after all?"

"I have very little doubt on that score. I marked the spot when we called this afternoon."

"Well, I'll take your word for it. What about the girl?"

"She didn't bite."

"Just as well. Personally, I think that was the weakest part of the whole scheme. I still don't see how you could have got the girl off in the boat, and given them the slip yourself."

"I should have found a way. But why discuss a situation which will not occur? Tell me your own news—has anything happened to you?"

"I hung on to that young fool for awhile," replied Beatrice, "fearing he'd follow you. He's one of the most curious boys I've ever struck."

"Well, I suppose you proved to yourself that there was no harm in him, or he'd never have given you the slip, eh?"

"I did let him give me the slip," she admitted, "but I'm wishing now that I hadn't."

"Well, forget him. I'm going to get some rest, and I advise you to do the same. There won't be much sleep for either of us, Beatrice, tonight."

The hours dragged by. Dinner-time came. Afterwards, they smoked and chatted, and retired early to their room. Geoffrey threw himself on the couch, and closed his eyes. He appeared to be sleeping, and he did not open his eyes again till the clock struck half an hour after midnight. He had not slept a wink.

He found Beatrice standing beside the sofa. She had her hat and coat on. Without a word, they slipped from the room, down the soft-carpeted stairs, and out through the front door. Then they separated.

With a strangely beating heart, Geoffrey crept through the deserted roads towards Marine Row. It was an inky night. The sea lay under the stars like a black cloak. Looking inland, there might have been fields or houses or mountains, for all one could see.

Every now and again, he used his electric torch to mark his direction. He acted with caution, in obedience to instinct, but there was no need for it. No one would have accosted him—yet.

Presently he came to a little back street running parallel with Marine Row, on which the gardens abutted. Only an easily ne-gotiated fence divided the gardens from the road. Geoffrey had no difficulty in finding the garden to No. 22. He had previously marked it. Five seconds later, he was inside.

A low hoot, not unlike that of an owl, came from the shrub-beries. He replied to the call. Joe Flipp, the dwarf, sidled out.

"All right?" whispered Joe.

"All in perfect order," Geoffrey whispered back.

Then they waited, crouching in the protection of the bushes, though this was an extra precaution, since the night itself had cast a complete shadow over all. Looking up, however, they could dimly see the roofs of the houses silhouetted against the spangled sky, and before long they noticed that the silhouette was punctured by a tiny spot of yellow. The spot disappeared, and then reappeared again, travelling along the roofs towards them.

"Tapley," whispered the dwarf, "now we're for it!"

Presently the light disappeared for good, and a faint, swishing sound was heard on the roof above them. That was all they heard. Tapley knew his job. The window through which he slipped was negotiated soundlessly, and they heard nothing more until a door opened some six feet off, and a voice whispered:

"*Seventy-one.*"

"Twenty-six," whispered the dwarf.

"Forty-nine," whispered Geoffrey.

By which replies, Edward Tapley knew he was among friends.

They passed into the house, closing the door after them, and making, with scarcely a sound, for the front sitting-room on the first floor. But, quiet though they were, many concealed listeners heard them.

"I'll lead," whispered Geoffrey, as they came to the stairs.

"Of course," muttered Tapley. "You always do."

"Shurrup," said the dwarf, digging him with his elbow.

Creeping up the narrow stairs in single file, they reached the door of the front sitting-room, and Geoffrey softly turned the handle. A sudden fear seized him that those who were hidden would reveal themselves too soon, or that some incautious member would give himself away. But Hobson knew his job too well for that. He had picked his men, and he realized, as he held his breath behind a curtain, that this must be a waiting game.

It was, nevertheless, an agonizing one for him, and he felt as though his heart would burst.

"*Now then—where?*" whispered the voice of Joe Flipp.

"Hist!" replied the voice of Geoffrey Mordaunt.

They listened, but not a sound was heard. They waited for five seconds, which seemed an eternity, and then Edward Tapley repeated Joe's question.

"Come on—we're wasting time," he exclaimed, in a low tone. "Where's the ruby?"

"*There,*" murmured Geoffrey Mordaunt, softly.

He pointed to a wall.

"Wotcher mean? That's a wall!"

"Joe Flipp, you're a genius," replied Geoffrey, softly. "I believe it is a wall."

"Shurrup!" spat Joe. "Blimy if I knows what you're gettin' at."

"You will, before you're much older. I will show you the prettiest hiding-place that was ever devised. Patience. Go to that wall, Tapley. And you, too, Joe. Go to it, and examine it where I throw my light."

He flashed his torch, as he spoke, and the two men advanced to the wall, peering at it closely.

"You will see a new strip of wall-paper there," whispered Geoffrey, clearly and distinctly; and none of the ears for which his words were intended lost a word. "It has been put there, by the landlady, to cover up a bullet-hole. A bullet-hole fired at close range. A bullet-hole made, my friend, by Baxter one second after he knocked the lamp over. You observe, a lamp is now on the pedestal, near to the spot. Baxter had a *brain*, my lads— and it took another brain to interpret his ingenuity."

"You mean—'e slipped it through the hole into the wall?"

"That is exactly what I do mean. Pull the paper off, and, unless I am very much mistaken, you will find it is the door to the ruby. The ruby has probably slipped down some way, so we'll have to get busy."

Tapley was already tearing the paper off, and the dwarf, whose head just reached the spot, got out his knife.

"Hist—what's that?" cried Geoffrey, suddenly. "Outside— quick!"

It was the signal. Chaos began. Figures darted from the curtains, and came hurrying along the passage. Flash-lights gleamed, and revolver shots rang out. For ten seconds, utter confusion reigned.

Then, the oaths and the struggles ceased, and only heavy breathing broke the silence as someone lit the lamp. Three men stood, handcuffed, before half a dozen police officials—Edward Tapley, Joe Flipp, and Geoffrey Mordaunt.

Geoffrey Mordaunt was ready for most emergencies, but he was not prepared for the look of fury which was hurled at him by the young detective who faced him.

"By God, I've caught you!" he cried, in a voice choking with emotion.

"It looks like it," replied Geoffrey, coolly.

A month ago, he and this young detective had worked shoulder to shoulder.

"And, if you're the man I think you are, you'll swing for it!"

"There, we differ."

Wilfred Hobson controlled himself with an effort. His next words rang out sharp and crisp.

"Is one of your names Mr Dicks?" he demanded.

"It wouldn't surprise me," replied Geoffrey.

"Then, by Heaven—"

One of the other officials laid his hand on Hobson's shoulder.

"I know how you're feeling, sir," he said, in a quiet, respectful voice. "It's a blow to all of us. But perhaps—"

"You're right," replied Hobson. "Nevertheless, I've got to tell this man what I think of him. You're a devil in human shape —a black spot in humanity—a curse! By your foul acts, you've driven men to ruin and insanity, if you haven't killed them with your own hands. And now, to crown all, you've prostrated the sweetest girl I've ever had the honour of knowing by killing, in cold blood, her fiancé, Geoffrey Mordaunt."

So it had leaked out at last. Geoffrey closed his eyes for a moment. The sight of that young face, driven to frenzy by his own death, and accusing him of it, was more than he could stand. And, divided from him by a few walls and feet of space, Joan lay mourning him.

Temptation seized him—the temptation to proclaim himself, and to relieve the sufferings of his two faithful friends. He hesitated.

"Who robbed me of the satisfaction of capturing this fiend? Who handcuffed him?" Hobson asked.

Then Geoffrey suddenly woke up. No, he would not give up. He would go on, while the power was still his.

"I did!" he shouted, flinging the bogus handcuffs from him.

The handcuffs crashed into the lamp, upsetting it. Once more, confusion reigned. Geoffrey hurled himself out of the room, and, finding the key on the outside, locked the door. Angry cries were raised on the other side of the door, but he did not wait to hear them. In a trice he was down the stairs, out in the back garden, and over the wall. He had a good start, and he knew where a motorcar was waiting for him.

"Drive like hell," he said to Beatrice, when he reached her.

Beatrice complied. For two minutes, no word was spoken, while the panting man collected himself. The sense of ease, the rapid motion, the vital feminine presence by his side, filled him with a strange, unconquerable elation.

"What's happened?" asked the woman coolly.

She had nerve.

"The worst," replied Geoffrey. "They're caught."

"Blockheads!"

"You express my sentiments exactly."

There was a silence.

"What about the ruby?" asked Beatrice, suddenly.

"I expect the police are putting my theory to the test at this moment. I did not wait to hear the result."

"Well, what's it matter," said the woman, after a pause, "so long as they didn't catch you? When shall we quit, John, and settle down?"

A figure shot out into the road.

"Steady," murmured Geoffrey.

"See if I can hit him," replied Beatrice.

The figure waved its arms wildly. The car raced onwards.

"Good Lord, the idiot's got a revolver!" exclaimed Geoffrey. "It's a hold-up! Drive through him, and duck!"

But, to his astonishment, the car suddenly shrieked under the application of brakes. It groaned, and slowed, and stopped, with the figure still ten feet off.

"I believe I'm going to faint! Hold me tight!" murmured Beatrice, with wide, dilating eyes. "It's Baxter!"

CHAPTER 8

Necessity quickens the brain. Before the advent of Baxter, Geoffrey Mordaunt had felt himself slipping into a luxurious apathy without the mental strength to fight against it. Weary from the events of the day, suffering still from the complex emotions which had assailed him at the climax, and terribly close to that feminine comfort which raises sex above individuality and can make a man rest his tired head against a bosom he hates, he had sat beside Beatrice while she drove the car furiously through the night in a sort of stupor. But now, with the abrupt introduction of a new problem, the detective's mental faculties awoke, and he found himself absorbing all the details, in so far as they presented themselves, with that alertness which was second nature to him. And, while his mind worked, he subconsciously rejoiced in his release from temporary subjection.

What were the details? They were startling enough. Baxter, to whom Joe Flipp had passed on the ruby, who had fled from the police at Littlehampton under the *alias* of A. P. Smith, and who had committed suicide when capture looked imminent, had suddenly sprung before them, brandishing a revolver, and very much alive.

Geoffrey had never seen Baxter, and only knew him by repute. But for Beatrice's exclamation, he would have had no knowledge of the man's identity, and he thanked Beatrice grimly in his mind for having rendered one further service to him. Certainly, the small quiet-looking man whose expression of desperate sternness was now changing to one of profound astonishment did not appear as though he belonged to a crim-

inal gang. He had the outward appearance of a not very successful commercial traveller, with refined instincts and a perfectly
respectable outlook on life.

While these impressions flashed through Geoffrey's brain, he
was already forming his immediate plan of action. One point
was obvious, and he acted on it. Baxter's necessity was as great
as their own, or he would not have attempted to hold up a
motor-car. In a sharp, authoritative voice, Geoffrey called out:

"Quick! Get in!"

"By all the devils—" began Baxter, but Geoffrey cut him short.

"We've no time to call on devils," he said, curtly. "Jump in.
Take the seat behind us. Will you drive on, Beatrice, or shall I?"

Beatrice regained her composure as quickly as Geoffrey had
regained his own. Again Geoffrey found himself trying to crush
his grudging admiration of her. As the car began to gather speed
again, he spoke to the man behind him, but without turning his
head.

"If you've anything vital to say at the Moment," he said, "say
it. Otherwise, keep it till a better time. We're in a hurry."

"So'm I," muttered Baxter. "Explanations can wait."

Geoffrey nodded. "Good. Then let her rip."

The moon was rising, and Beatrice made the most of it. But,
if it gave any assistance to the hares, it would be of equal assistance to the hounds, and, on the whole, Beatrice would have
preferred darkness. She was a skilful driver, and this was not the
first time she had led the police a dance. Presently she said:

"See anything?"

"No," answered Geoffrey. "But all the local stations will be no-
tified by now, I expect, so we're not out of the wood."

"Don't worry," replied Beatrice, coolly. "We'll beat them."

The moon flashed on her hair, silvering the auburn edges that
escaped from her close-fitting hat. Her eye was clear and steady,
and a faint smile of elation lit up her face. It was the smile of a
clever woman, enjoying her test. Geoffrey glanced at her, with
an odd expression.

"You like this game?" he asked.

"There's only one game I'll exchange it for," she retorted.

"Is it a respectable game?"

"One day," she flashed back, "you and I will go to church together every Sunday."

"I am afraid that day is very long distant."

"Perhaps. But it could be next week, if you'd say the word."

"You mean—you could give up all this—for me?"

"I believe I could, damn you," she replied.

"Still, one never knows till one tries, does one?"

Geoffrey glanced behind him. Baxter's eyes were closed. Suddenly he stiffened. His quick ears had caught an unmistakable sound.

"They're after us, Beatrice," he said.

"That's a long way from catching us," she responded, and turned suddenly into a dark lane. "I expect my geography's as good as theirs."

"What would you do, if they caught us?"

"I never worry myself trying to answer impossible questions. What would *you* do, if the King turned a Socialist?"

Geoffrey smiled, but the smile did not last. The sound of the pursuing motor was still in his ears.

A sudden impulse seized him to end it all. Here were Baxter, Beatrice Fullerton, and himself. If he took the wheel, he could easily engineer matters so that they were captured. It would be a good haul. And, afterwards, he could hurry to Joan Heather's side, and put her out of her agony. He actually bent towards Beatrice, with the intention of replacing her, but another impulse held him back. There were better hauls ahead, if he held on.

"Damn," murmured Beatrice under her breath.

"What's the matter?" asked Geoffrey. "Listen. They're gaining. They must have a powerful car."

Geoffrey nodded. Perhaps, after all, the Fates were deciding matters for him. As the pursuing car could be heard more and more distinctly, he began to realize that the chase would probably end in their capture; and, with the perversity of human nature, the thought chafed him. A moment ago he had longed for capture, and had even thought seriously of engineering it. Now, in his new mood, it angered him to think that circumstances were leading him towards the goal of his former weakness. He realized, too, the dangers of a capture in this form. A stray shot might easily find him, and then Joan Heather would have to mourn him in actual fact.

Beatrice dodged and turned, gave the car all she could stand, and engineered every resource with wonderful skill. The odds, however, were too big against her. Presently, with a queer gleam in her eye, she turned to Geoffrey.

"We're going to be beaten, John," she said, "unless we change our tactics. Things look ugly."

"They do," replied Geoffrey Mordaunt, and turned round to Baxter. His eyes were still closed. "Wake up, Baxter! You may be going to a longer sleep soon."

Baxter opened his eyes suddenly.

"Dear me!" he said, quietly. "Have I been asleep?"

"You have."

"Then it's the first sleep I've had for two nights. What's happening?"

"We're being caught—that's what's happening," Beatrice informed him. "It's going to be a case of revolvers. Get yours ready."

Geoffrey eyed her, frowning.

"Now, perhaps, you will answer my question a little less frivolously," he said. "What will you do—if we are caught?"

"Fire all my bullets but one," she answered.

"And that one?"

"Oh, I'll keep that for myself, if necessary."

"You couldn't face it, then?" he mused.

"What? Respectability between prison walls?" She laughed scornfully. "No, thank you! If I ever become good, I must receive my price." Her lips assumed a cynical curl. "You know, John, people regard death much too seriously. You've said so yourself. And respectability—again these are your own words—can cause such a pleasant little hell all of its own that it's a wonder more people don't drift out of it—either to our own kind of hell or the momentary agony of pulling a trigger."

"Is that your philosophy, then?"

"No—it's yours. You taught it to me." Hardly realizing it, Geoffrey found himself defending his dead brother.

"Perhaps you were a willing learner?" he suggested, ironically.

"Oh, I was. You have taught me many things. And now I am going to teach you one."

They were passing through a wide, wood-bordered road, and the pursuing car was still steadily gaining on them. Suddenly, Beatrice applied her brakes and, turning sharply to the right, plunged into the woods.

The car leapt and jolted. It crashed through a gap in a small hedge, and plunged into a clump of tall, straight trees.

"What the devil are you doing?" cried Baxter, leaping out.

Geoffrey, too, gave a hurried jump. It was a narrow shave. Beatrice, unable to jump, received the worst shaking, but she escaped without serious injury, and soon stood beside them, regarding the damaged car. For a few moments they merely panted, and counted their bruises. Then Baxter repeated his question.

"What the devil was that for?" he demanded.

"The reason should be obvious to you," replied Geoffrey, who had quickly divined Beatrice's plan. "Now then. Revolvers ready, and find a hiding-place on the other side of the road."

"You always were quick in the uptake," smiled Beatrice.

They hurried across the road, and were only just in time. They had hardly settled themselves before the pursuing car came into view and grew bigger and bigger as it raced along its course.

Suddenly, one of the occupants gave a shout, and the driver slowed up. They had seen the spot where the track of their quarry's wheels had veered abruptly to right angles, and, in another instant, they saw the wrecked car.

"Steady," whispered Geoffrey, to his companions. "Not a shot unless it's necessary, or until I give the word."

Six men, headed by Wilfred Hobson, were already in the road, and making their way cautiously towards the wood where the derelict car could be seen wedged among the trees. And as they stalked cautiously forward, with revolvers ready, three other figures began approaching the car in the road from the other side, with equal stealth. The driver alone remained in the car, and his eyes were glued on the backs of his companions. He was listening for the first shot, and secretly wishing that he had followed his mother's advice and become a baker. But who would have thought that a course of lessons in motoring could ever have led to this?

His heart beat fast, to his annoyance. He recalled that, during the war, he had become more or less hardened to this sort of thing. Often, then, he had been on guard, straining his ears for sounds at times when he was not being deafened by them, listening for signals, hearing queer rustlings that might be the forerunner of some swift death—

And then, suddenly, he gasped. For a second he actually thought he was back in Gallipoli as a hand was clapped over his mouth, and he felt the muzzles of two revolvers against him.

A voice in his ear whispered, fiercely:

"Drive on this instant, or you're a dead man!"

In a frenzy of fear the chauffeur obeyed. With the revolvers pressed meaningly against his body there seemed no other logical course open to him. He drove his new masters with all the zeal with which, five minutes ago, he had been pursuing them, and, before the men in the wood had realized the turn of events, their car was racing away from them and becoming a fast-diminishing point in the moonlit distance.

One or two ineffectual shots rang out. Then intercourse between the pursuers and the pursued ceased. Two miles were covered in silence.

"And now," said Geoffrey Mordaunt, "I am afraid we must get rid of you, my man."

"Damn you," chattered the chauffeur. "You'll all pay for this one day."

"Stop the car," proceeded Geoffrey, "and get out. It will be quite useless to feel for your revolver, for I have already taken possession of that, and your own revolver is covering you. Hurry, now!"

The trembling chauffeur, with further curses, obeyed. How right, he thought, mothers always are. Half a minute later he was standing in disconsolate loneliness by the road-side, shaking his fist at those who had imposed the necessity of a long night tramp.

Beatrice was again at the wheel. She was as good a driver as Geoffrey, and the arrangement suited the detective.

"What now?" she asked.

"I think we had better change our original destination," he replied. "Have you any preference, Baxter?"

"I don't mind where we go," answered Baxter, who was beginning to close his eyes again, "so long as it's a damned long way off."

"Then I suggest Brackleton," said Beatrice. "The moon's good, and I think I can make it in three hours—"

"I say, John," interposed Baxter, who was again in the back seat, "what's happened to that little scar that used to be at the back of your neck?"

Geoffrey turned round curtly.

"I think," he said, "this is hardly the time to discuss scars? But, if you want to know, I've found a way of blotting it out."

"That's interesting," yawned Baxter. "You must tell me how you did it some time—I've got one I'd rather like to get rid of. The police are too fond of scars, aren't they?"

He laughed, and closed his eyes again. Beatrice shot a glance at Geoffrey.

"I think he's a little light-headed," she said, in a low voice. "He's behaving very oddly. Well, what do you think about Brackleton?"

"It seems a good idea," assented Geoffrey, guardedly, "but why do you select it?"

"Well, it seems fairly obvious, doesn't it?" she exclaimed.

"Tobias may be there. And we haven't seen the Jowls for some while—you said we ought to look them up, you know. And then there's Jones."

"Geoffrey nodded. "You're right," he agreed, wondering who Jones might be. "Let it be Brackleton."

The car seemed to take new life with its new objective. Brackleton was not a new name to Geoffrey, but he knew little about it, for whenever it had been mentioned it had been referred to as a place of such obvious importance that to have appeared ignorant or too curious in regard to its significance would have ill fitted his new part. Something, evidently, was going on at Brackleton. It was a mysterious axis upon which much turned. There had been no mention of it in the accounts which had been drawn up during that first conference at the house in London, otherwise he might have been primed. As it was, he could only speculate and guess.

He tried to draw Beatrice into a communicative vein, but she was moody and taciturn, and began to show signs of fatigue. He dared not offer to drive, for he would not have known the way. Presently she told him bluntly that she was too tired to talk. Fearing that she might ask him to change places with her, he also allowed indications of a fatigue which was not entirely feigned to show themselves in his demeanour. Behind him Baxter snored.

Thus they proceeded in silence. Beatrice, now that all sign of pursuit was passed and their objective was fixed, settled down to her task in a spirit of dogged steadiness, and their powerful car devoured the white, moon-bleached road. Now they passed through great woods, where the light streamed through the trees in the form of a brilliant lace pattern; now they raced over silent moorland, where the low bushes cast stumpy velvet shadows, black pools in the silver heath-sea; now they went by star-spangled ponds, through villages devoid of cheerful yellow lights, by stately parks all ripe for ghosts. It was impossible not to feel some exultation in the ride, and once, when Beatrice looked towards him and caught his eye upon her, she gave a little triumphant laugh.

"Even hell's not so bad on a moonlight night, eh, John?" she said.

Resisting his impulse to be human, Geoffrey replied:

"You speak like a dissatisfied child. Hell is your own term. I hope you're not weakening, Beatrice?"

"Weakening?" she retorted, flashing. "Don't worry, John. I'm not weakening. I've got enough strength left to break you one day."

"Preserve it," answered Geoffrey. "You may need it."

"Sometimes I wonder," she said, after a short silence, "whether there is any real difference between intense love and intense hate."

Geoffrey answered her harshly.

"Love doesn't exist for people like you and me," he exclaimed. "We have passions, but they are not love. Love is——"

"Yes? What?"

"A fool's game," he said. "How many people who have loved you have found it so?"

"That's true—it is a fool's game," she replied; and silence fell again.

Only once in the long strange journey did they stop before it ended. They stopped in order that Geoffrey might alight and examine the engine. Beatrice swore that nothing was the matter, but Geoffrey insisted, and spent some minutes conducting the examination, while Beatrice fretted in her seat. Another car, proceeding in the opposite direction, pulled up outside an inn some little way beyond them. Geoffrey strolled across to the motorist, and returned almost immediately.

"What did you ask him?" demanded Beatrice.

"We're getting rather low in petrol," answered Geoffrey. "I asked if he could spare any, but he couldn't."

Then they proceeded on their way, and the motorist turned to look after them. He was not thinking of petrol. Petrol, as a matter of fact, had not been mentioned during the very brief interview. He was wondering, vaguely, why the man who had come up to him had looked so anxious and worried while asking him whether he was on the right road to Brackleton.

"Funny how you get feelin's about things," murmured the motorist, "but I could swear, by the look in his eye, that that feller's been up to some mischief!"

CHAPTER 9

"Another half-hour, and we'll be there," announced Beatrice, coming out of a reverie. "Get ready for bumps."

They were no longer driving through a moon-lit land. Cocks were trying their voices, and a dull glow on the horizon had already succeeded the cold grey light that sullenly precedes the dawn. The country showed another change as well. It was no longer neat and well-ordered, but had a rugged wildness, as though the tangled trees and bushes around them held domain against the levelling hand of progress. They proved the outposts of wilder, thicker woods, towards which the car now made its tortuous way through rutted roads and narrow, over-grown lanes.

Geoffrey nodded, in reply to Beatrice's remark, feigning a familiarity with country which was actually new to him. He turned in his seat, and saw that the bumping had awakened Baxter.

"Well, Baxter," he said, "let's have your story now. There'll be plenty of other things to talk about when we get inside, so well clear the ground first with you."

"How much of it do you know?" asked Baxter.

"Just as much as the papers have described," replied Geoffrey.

"That doesn't tell *me* much," answered Baxter, "because there are no paper-shops where I've been. You know that I had to escape from Littlehampton, of course?"

"Yes, and Joe told us all the events that led up to your flight. That was a clever idea of yours, slipping the ruby into the wall."

"Ah, you got on to that!" exclaimed Baxter, with professional pride. "It was the only thing I could think of."

"It was neat. But, unfortunately, your pains went for nothing. We found out what the police could not, and were caught—last night, just before you held us up—as we were on the point of looking into your hiding-place."

"Who were caught?"

"Joe Flipp and Edward Tapley. They nearly got me, too, but I just managed to give them the slip. Of course, by this time the police have got the ruby, and, thanks to all your bungling, one of the finest chances we ever had is lost. Twenty thousand pounds gone! Well, what about you? It was reported that you were shot."

Baxter smiled. It was not a particularly nice smile.

"That wasn't true," he said.

"But the body was found, and taken to the police station."

"*My* body wasn't found. I'm afraid I had to adopt rather drastic tactics. I was up a dark lane when they fired at me, and the bullet did graze me. But the fellow they found was a man I shot myself, at the same moment, just as he was coming at me from the other direction. They thought they'd winged me when they came upon him, for I was well out of the way by then. Whether they still think that, or whether they've simply kept up the pretence to put me off my guard, I don't know. Anyway, I was pretty ill afterwards, and have been hiding ever since."

"It sounds quite plausible," commented Geoffrey. "The only thing that remains is to tell us why you held us up."

"I had no money, no food, and was desperate. I was too weak to dodge about on my feet much more, and felt that I must get clear at once, or it would be all up. My plan was to motor up to London and try and find you—and there you were, all the time." He closed his eyes again. "Too tired to talk any more. Better after breakfast."

"H'm," said Geoffrey. "It's hanging, if they get you."

"Of course it is," yawned Baxter." That's why I was desperate."

"Human life means little to me," proceeded Geoffrey, with a sharp note in his voice, "but it's quite clear that there has been a good deal of unnecessary killing lately. Are you all losing your nerve, or what is it? Joe'll hang, when James Cardhew's murder is brought home to him. So'll you, when your luck changes. You ask for it!"

He spoke angrily, using the formula which he imagined John might have used. But, if Baxter heard, he made no sign. Despite the increased jolting of the car, his eyes were fast closed.

By now the forest enveloped them utterly, and a dilapidated inn, which they had passed fifteen minutes ago, formed the last memory of a human habitation. But presently a chimney broke the ceaseless vistas of trees on their left, just where their lane gave up trying to be a lane, and ended, with a green sign, in grasses and moss. Here the three occupants of the car alighted, and Geoffrey found himself pervaded with an intense professional curiosity as to what he would find in that mysterious cottage tucked away among the trees and screened so effectively from prying eyes.

Evidently, it formed one of the meeting-places of the gang, for Tobias King, the big, boyish-looking man whose outward benignity shielded a soul of uncanny depths, was expected there, and the oft-mentioned Jowls, were evidently in residence. Beyond these bare facts, Geoffrey knew nothing of the cottage and its significance.

They walked to the porch, and, as they approached, Geoffrey saw that the building was somewhat larger than he had first imagined. He sized it up as a condemned cottage which had been ingeniously patched up and added to by a skilled hand, and for some particular purpose.

The door was opened by a large, sour-visaged man. He had an ample body, yet his arms and hands looked ample beyond proportion. A scraggy, sandy beard adorned his chin, and thin strands of similar-coloured hair made no attempt to beautify the top of his head. Altogether, thought Geoffrey Mordaunt, a most unprepossessing specimen of humanity, and evidently Mr Jowl. It would be delightful, further decided the detective, to be the means of despatching Mr Jowl to whatever end his career fitted him for.

Jowl gave him a surly look, and there was a quality in it which instantly decided Geoffrey on his line of action.

"Now, then, what are you staring at?" he demanded, curtly. "Haven't you ever seen a man before?"

"Who's staring?" growled Jowl.

"Get a move on!" answered Geoffrey. "We've been travelling all night, and are not in the sweetest of humours."

"Come in, sir, come in," cried a thin, sharp voice behind the portly frame of Mr Jowl. A small, bony woman, looking like a shrunken bird of prey, grew out of the interior darkness. "There's a fire in the parlour. You'll be wanting breakfast?"

"Yes, as quick as you can," interposed Beatrice. "Is Mr King here?"

"Not yet," responded the thin voice. "But we've another visitor." She cackled inanely, and Geoffrey cut her short.

"That's enough," he rasped out. "Listen, Jowl. This is the programme. Breakfast first. Then I want to talk to you. After that, see that rooms are ready for us. We shall need a rest."

Jowl nodded and disappeared, and, as the party made its way to the parlour, Beatrice whispered in Geoffrey's ear:

"You know best, of course—but I wouldn't be too short with Jowl. He's an unpleasant man."

"And knows the side his bread's buttered," replied Geoffrey. "Thank you, my dear, but I don't make mistakes."

She shrugged her shoulders, and a minute later they were sitting in a parlour which, despite the evil atmosphere of the place, was pleasant enough, and grew all the more pleasant as the table was spread and signs of a meal began to appear.

"Queer," thought Geoffrey Mordaunt, "what a human bond is human need! I despise these people, yet am content to eat with them, and to rest with them. Necessity levels us all. It is only when we are well and satisfied that the differences show."

Breakfast was eaten in silence. They absorbed themselves in it and Baxter made a frank pig of himself. But, afterwards, their tongues were loosened, and the Jowls were sent for.

"Now then," began Geoffrey, lighting a cigarette, "let's hear your news. Tell us all that's happened here."

"Nothing's happened," replied Jowl.

"Everything quiet, eh?"

"Yes."

"No one called?"

"No one called. No one been near the place since a fortnight, when *he* came." Jowl jerked his head towards the door.

Geoffrey nodded, with a curious tightening at his heart. "Well," he said, slowly, "and what about him?"

"Oh—just goes on the same. You'll see for yourself."

"And perhaps the sooner the better. Well, you're not over-communicative, Jowl. Perhaps *you've* a little more to say for yourself?" He turned to the small, bony woman at his side. "Let's hear your report."

She shook her head. She was as uncommunicative as her husband. "We don't get no Lord Mayors' Shows here," she observed with a simper. "It's a pleasure when we do see a face sometimes."

"The fewer the better," retorted Geoffrey. "Well, since you're neither of you exactly wells of information, let's see—the visitor. Coming, Beatrice?"

"No, thank you," she answered. "I'm going to sleep for eight hours, at least. Room ready, Mrs Jowl?"

"Aye," said that lady. "Everything's ready. I'll take you up now, if you like?"

"Thank you. And what about you, Jack?"

Geoffrey realized that this was the first time he had learned Baxter's first name.

"Oh, I'm all for a rest," he yawned. "Our guest doesn't appeal to me in the least."

Mr Jowl took charge of Geoffrey, while Mrs Jowl conducted the others to an upper storey.

"The Chief's in a funny mood," commented Mrs Jowl, as she led the way upstairs. "Ready to snap your head off!"

"Don't like him today," agreed Baxter. "Don't like him. Not one little bit."

"Well, take my advice, and don't cross him," said Beatrice.

"He's a puzzling devil, but we'd miss him if anything happened."

"That's what *I* say," interposed the bony woman. "That's what *I* say. Jim thinks different. He don't like all this waiting. Talks about ending it all, and going to Australia. 'But how are you going to *get* there?' I ask. Why, there's only one man could manage that, and we all know who he is, don't we?"

"You're quite a sensible woman, Mrs Jowl," replied Beatrice. "If you remain so, and keep a curb on your husband, you'll both end your days in comfort yet—that I'll promise you. But you can't do big things without money, can you? And does your husband know how to get that? Trust the Chief."

"H'm—I'm not so sure," murmured Baxter. "He seems to have bungled Littlehampton."

"And what about *your* bungling?" demanded Beatrice. "You made a nice mess of things!"

"Well, I'll forgive him," said Baxter, "if he'll show me how to get rid of that scar of his. I'm going to have one on my shoulder that will mark me as Jack Baxter for the rest of my life."

Meanwhile, the subject of their conversation was staring at a young, pale-faced man, sitting in a comfortable arm-chair with his legs crossed. The only notable points about the room he was seated in were that it had only one door, a very substantial one, and that the lighting arrangements were somewhat unsatisfactory. The window was a small one, and quite inaccessible.

"Good morning," said the pale young man. "This is a pleasure."

"I'm glad you think so," replied Geoffrey, studying him. "But you've a little more to say to me than that, haven't you?"

"A damned sight more," exclaimed the young man; but subsided as suddenly as he had fired up. "No, I've promised myself that I'll not get excited, so you needn't think you're going to make me. Ask that ugly face there how I've behaved myself!"

Jowl grunted.

"Well," said Geoffrey, "you can tell me things without flaring up. Maybe you'll find me in a new mood."

"And maybe not."

"As you say, and maybe not. But changes do occur sometimes,

you know, even in the worst-regulated families, and perhaps, if you get your load off your chest, we may find some solution."

The pale young man began to study Geoffrey with a new interest.

"A compromise, eh? Is that your game?"

"I have said nothing about a compromise."

"No, you haven't. And perhaps I'm not in a mood for a compromise myself. I'll tell you what my terms are. Here goes. First, I've got to be let free. Second, I've got to horsewhip the ugly brute—"

"Has he been treating you roughly?" asked Geoffrey, glancing at Jowl.

"No, I've not—yet," replied Jowl. "But he knows this game can't go on for ever. I hate waiting."

"Nevertheless, you'll wait, my friend, just as long as I tell you to. I know how to play my cards." He turned to the captive once more. "Go on with your list. What's the third item?"

"The third item is that not a cent of my money shall you have. It's mine, by right of possession—by the same right that you make yours. And lastly—that horsewhip again. There's one more person I'm going to use it on."

He paused, and Geoffrey asked him who that might be.

"Beatrice Fullerton," he cried, fiercely. "The woman who decoyed me here. I'm going to spoil her beauty! Is she here?"

Geoffrey did not answer. A sensation of nausea came over him. For a few moments he had imagined that this young man was some innocent victim. That he had been victimized was clear. His attitude, however, did not suggest much innocence.

Perhaps Beatrice Fullerton deserved horse-whipping? As the question rose in his mind, he realized that she deserved very much more than this, and that the question had only occurred to him as a result of the partial spell she had cast over him— a spell which, he told himself over and over again, had nothing fundamental in it, but was assisted by the general demoralization of his surroundings and the decadent moods he had to assume. Yet, despite all, he could not contemplate with equanimity the picture of this young man meting out moral justice to Beatrice. There is little nobility in the vision of one scamp chastising another.

Acting on his now common practice of searching John's soul for guidance through the underworld, Geoffrey suddenly realized the course John would have taken, and he adopted it.

"I haven't time to waste now," he said, "but I'll make you an offer. Come in with us. You've a sharp brain, you've pluck, and you've common-sense. Let us have possession of this money, but share yourself in its final distribution. Give it to the common purse. We're out for big things, you know, and you'll do better with us than on your own."

"I'm damned if I'd trust you," muttered the young man, but Geoffrey could see that the idea had some interest for him.

"Well, think it over. And don't be too rash in your determination to spoil Beatrice Fullerton's beauty. Suppose it were used in your interests instead of against them? Would you feel the same about her?"

"Perhaps not," admitted the young man, while Geoffrey inwardly cursed him.

"Well, think it over," said Geoffrey, turning to go. "And remember this. You may talk big—just as big as you like. But there's only one alternative to the offer I have made, and the alternative is that you will be smashed to very, very small morsels."

This peroration did not entirely rejoice the pale young man, but it went straight to the heart of Mr Jowl. For the first time that worthy smiled.

Up in his room Geoffrey sank down on his bed and closed his eyes. But it was a long while before sleep came, despite his utter weariness. His problems, practical and human, were becoming too complex for perfect rest, and they crowded into his mind while his physical needs tried to send them packing. Added to these things was the strange atmosphere of the house itself, its haunting setting, and utter loneliness. Amid this wilderness of trees there should have been peace; and peace, in one sense, there was; but it was a brooding, malignant peace, throbbing with subconscious discord.

What a motley of folk to slumber among! Baxter, who was wanted for murder. The pale young man downstairs—evidently Jones—who appeared to have plenty of crimes to his calendar. Mr and Mrs Jowl, as unsavoury a pair of caretakers as he had ever come across. Beatrice Fullerton, cruel, unscrupulous, beautiful, and wanting his love. And Tobias King, on his way!

But sleep did come at last, and, when it came, it came fully. When he opened his eyes it was half-past four in the afternoon. He jumped up quickly from his bed, refreshed and alert again; and, after a hurried toilet, went out into the passage.

The house was quiet. He could not hear anyone stirring. Had anything happened while he slept? Disturbing possibilities occurred to him. Quietly he went downstairs, hardly knowing what he expected, yet primed for any event or discovery. When he opened the door of the sitting-room and found Beatrice quietly sipping tea, the sight gave him a sense of absurd comfort and relief for which his supersensitiveness instantly reviled himself. He was shocked to discover that, already, he could find impulsive pleasure in an undisturbed criminal routine.

Beatrice looked up as he entered, and smiled. She might at that moment have been a charming hostess welcoming a guest to tea in some eminently respectable country house.

"Ah, John," she said. "How nice of you to break up my loneliness."

He sat down beside her, and took the cup of tea she poured out for him.

"Any news?" he asked.

"No," she answered.

"Where are the others?"

"Baxter is still sleeping in his room. Mr Jowl has been out in the wood all the afternoon, chopping or something. His charming wife is in the kitchen. And Jones—so I understand, I haven't been to see him—is still eating his heart out behind a locked door. I, at least, am communicative."

"You are. Thank you."

"I realize, if others don't, the necessity for keeping you in touch with unimportant details. You owe me some gratitude, you know, John."

"I hope I am not ungrateful," he said, grudgingly.

"Oh no—you shower bouquets upon me. This morning I have taken your side against Mr Baxter and Mr Jowl."

"You know where your interest lies then, if they don't."

"I am quite sure that one day I shall kill you, my dear," replied Beatrice coolly, "and, when I do, you won't exactly like it."

"Thank you for the warning. Now let me give you one. Jones is quite as anxious to kill you as you are to kill me."

"He told you that?"

"He implied it. But the horsewhip, I think, comes first." She flushed slightly. "Tell me, Beatrice," he asked curiously, "how far do you go with your victims? How far did you go with this young man?"

"His present agony," she responded lightly, "may be traced to a single kiss."

"And are you proud of these conquests?" he went on.

She looked at him quizzically for a moment before she replied. Then she said: "Professionally, perhaps, yes. But they have no other interest for me."

"Nor, I take it, has the fate of your victims?"

"The victim is usually my own sex," she retorted. "It is we who generally have to suffer agony for unwise impulses." She laughed suddenly. "Damn you, John, why are you so serious this afternoon? You're making me talk like a fool. I wish you could realize how cordially I detest you!" She threw her arms behind her back and mocked him. "Yes, detest you. You are quite right —I only defended you this morning because I know where the butter is."

"And I defended you for just the same reason," replied Geoffrey Mordaunt. "When Jones talked about thrashing you, and started cursing your beauty, I suggested that he might bless your beauty instead of cursing it if he joined with us. That would turn him into a friend instead of an enemy."

"Neat idea," she conceded, as she refilled his cup, "but I think I prefer Master Jones as an enemy."

A step outside interrupted their discourse. Mrs Jowl came hurrying in.

"I've seen 'em up the lane!" she exclaimed.

"Who?" demanded Geoffrey, rising quickly.

"Mr King. He's coming along now. And—I think he's bringing another visitor!"

"Well, well, don't get so excited about it, woman!" cried Geoffrey, testily. "Go and let them in! You ought to be used to visitors by now."

But had Mrs Jowl been gifted with second-sight she would have seen that the Chief's excitement, beneath the surface, was hardly less than her own. Another visitor! What fresh villainy was he about to encounter in this criminal nest? He began to realize that he had no definite plan, and that, if he wished to repeat his former success, he must stir himself and do some furious thinking. Uniformed Respectability must be led to this spot, and with little delay. But how? How?

And, even as the plan was forming in his brain, and the first details were being rapidly arranged, a fresh problem was approaching up the passage. The door opened, and in walked Mr Tobias King, with his hand firmly grasped on the shoulder of Joan Heather.

CHAPTER 10

Wilfred Hobson had passed through many periods of perplexity. They came to every detective, however successful, in the course of his duties—periods when the mists they are striving to pierce swallow up theories and make facts vanish. Sometimes the mists are dissipated, if the detective is fortunate and is skilful at his job; at other times, the fog remains permanent, and the detective admits himself beaten.

The fog which now confronted Hobson seemed of the permanent kind, and as he sat in his room at Littlehampton, exerting all his efforts to pierce it, a heavy weight hung over him. The news that Geoffrey Mordaunt was dead, coupled with his failure to capture the man responsible for his death, imparted lines to Hobson's face which did not in the least fit his late part of holiday lounger. He looked, this morning, a different being—a grim, determined being, temporarily at bay.

For the hundredth time, he ran over the events of the past few hours in his mind. He visualized the extraordinary scene of the escape, the battering on the locked door, the subsequent opening of the door, and the chase that had followed. More than one party had set out, but his own alone had been successful in picking up the threads, and gradually the chased car had been overtaken. And then, with a wave of anger, he visualized the scene in the wood, when he had been duped by a simple trick, and had been ignominiously forced to walk back to Littlehampton with his party.

At Littlehampton, a further disappointment had met him. A stone had indeed been found in the wall at No. 22 Marine Row, but the stone was a sham one, and, if the genuine stone had in fact been stolen from James Cardhew at the time of his death, it was still in the hands of the thieves. The two prisoners remained moody and silent. If they had anything to reveal, they refused to reveal it.

Hobson tried to piece the matter together in his mind. There were various theories. One was that the man known as Smith, who had been chased out of Littlehampton and had apparently been shot, still had the ruby on him. The police had at first believed that the body they had come upon was the body of the fugitive, but later—as Baxter himself had surmised—had realized their mistake, while considering it temporarily unwise to make the error public. If the fugitive thought they were duped, they argued sagaciously, he would be less careful than if he realized that they were still searching for him.

But, according to Hobson's first theory regarding the ruby, Smith would have had two rubies on his person—a sham one and a real one. Was it not more probable that the man had himself been duped?—that no real ruby had been stolen from James Cardhew at all? Carrying the matter back a step further, James Cardhew may never have possessed a genuine stone, and the whole tragedy may have revolved around a worthless imitation!

Everything had been done that was possible; strings had been pulled, and approved accounts of the previous night's events had been sent to the press. The morning's papers had missed most of the tide, but the early afternoons had come in for the full flood of it, and were making the most of it on their posters. Looking out of his window, Hobson saw the words: "Search for Motor Car," in big black type. It was his own car they were searching for, the car in which the fugitives had made their final escape into the impenetrable mist.

Hobson was just deciding to organize a visit to James Cardhew's house on the outskirts of Littlehampton when an official knocked on his door, and said they had a man whom they would like him to see. The young detective jumped up immediately, with the light of hope in his eyes. He knew that any clue, however slight, might prove all-revealing.

The man was a motorist, and he began by apologizing to Hobson for probably wasting his time.

"I don't think I've got much to tell you," he said, "but, when I read the accounts of this affair, I thought I had a bit of information that might be worth following up."

"Go ahead," replied Hobson. "Very good of you."

"Not at all. Well, here's my story, such as it is. Motoring's my business, and I had to deliver a car by ten o'clock this morning, so I've been motoring all night. Early in the morning—"

"What time?" interposed Hobson.

"Oh, I couldn't say, exactly. Four o'clock, p'raps. I'd pulled up for a moment, when I saw another car on the opposite side of the road. There were three people in it. A man is examining the engine. Presently he comes across to me, and asks, 'Am I right for Brackleton?' Never having heard of Brackleton, I tell him I don't know. Back he goes, and that's about all. Hardly worth mentioning, I daresay."

"But you must have had some special reason for mentioning it?" queried Hobson.

"Why, yes. The car seemed to be the exact kind of car described in my paper here, and I thought, as soon as the man spoke to me, that he was a wrong 'un. Funny how you get those feelings, isn't it? But he gave me that idea strongly. I can describe him to you, if you like."

"Please do so," said Hobson, eagerly.

The description which followed was, to Hobson, like a tonic to a sick man. His eye lit up as he recognized its details. Then he questioned the man more precisely about the time, and the spot where the meeting had taken place, and also about the other occupants of the car.

"You think there's anything in it?" asked the motorist, after he had been sucked dry.

"I think there is so much in it," answered Hobson, "that I'm going to Brackleton right away."

"Do you think—if he is your man—that he might have asked

for Brackleton to put us off the scent?"

"He might," admitted Hobson, "but I've got to risk that. You can't pick and choose when you've only got one clue to go upon."

He thanked the motorist, and then made hurried plans. He found that the quickest way was by motor. While the motor being got ready, he ran round to tell Joan Heather the news. To his astonishment, he found that Joan had left.

"Left!" exclaimed Hobson. "But—surely it was very sudden?"

"Very sudden, sir! So I ses to myself," agreed the landlady. "But it ain't none o' my business. A stout gentleman calls—a friend or a relation or somethink—and, after next to no time, so it seems, sir, 'er bag's packed, and off they goes."

"Did she say she was coming back?

"She didn't seem to know."

"I don't like the look of it," said Hobson, frowning.

"Oh, that's all right," the landlady replied. "She paid up proper."

"I didn't mean that," retorted Hobson.

"I meant—it's surprising she should have left like that without a word to me."

"Ah, that's funny, now! I'd forgotten. I 'eard 'er say they was goin' to see you But, as you don't know nothink about it, I suppose they didn't, after all."

Hobson's anxiety grew. The fact that she had intended to tell him of her movements and had failed to do so suggested the worst possibilities. His joy in the hope of solving one problem was greatly dampened by the sudden introduction of another. However, there was nothing to be done beyond reporting the matter to head-quarters, and then getting ahead with his own programme.

About six hours later, at a dilapidated, tree-encircled inn, two men sat drinking at separate tables. One was a horsy-looking fellow, with check trousers and side-whiskers, and the other was a pedlar, whose only wares seemed to be shoe-laces. They drank for a while in silence, but presently the pedlar, who had been closely watched by the horsy individual, grew bold, and edged nearer.

"Buy a lace, sir?" he whined.

"No, thanks," replied the horsy man. "How do you expect to sell laces in a district like this, what?" The pedlar stared at him stupidly. "Expect to find customers among the trees, eh?"

"Wotcher getting' at?" retorted the tramp, disgustedly. He turned to the innkeeper, a sleepy fellow with very light hair. "Wot's the matter with the people about 'ere?"

"What d'yer mean, what's the matter with 'em?" answered the innkeeper. "What's the matter with you's more like it!" And he laughed at his joke.

"Same everywhere I goes!" mumbled the pedlar. "Nothing but kicks. Larst 'ouse I called at—Lummy, I thort they'd eat me up, I did!"

"Oh, where was that?" asked the horsy man.

"In the wood. Lorst meself, I 'ad, and come upon it orl of a sudden. ''Allo' I ses, 'little bit of orl rite. Fancy findin' a 'ouse 'ere,' I ses. And up I goes—"

"'Ere, we ain't pertickler interested in your Story," interrupted the innkeeper. "If you've finished your drink, you can 'op it."

"'Op it! That's right! Always told to 'op it," growled the pedlar. "That's wot they sed at the other place. Only they ses it like this. ''Ere,' they ses, 'wot are you doin'? This is privit,' they ses, 'and we don't want you to come pokin' yer nose round. Don't you never come 'ere no more,' they ses. 'Rich people's orl the same,' I ses. 'Rich?' they ses, 'wot makes you think we're rich?' And then I points to their car—"

"Man's loony," observed the innkeeper to the horsy individual.

"This certainly don't look like motorin' country," replied the latter.

"Course it ain't! There ain't no garages round 'ere." And again he laughed.

"Loony, am I?" cried the tramp indignantly. "Well, I could take yer straight ter a cottage *with* a garridge, so there! Bang in the middle of the wood—rummiest place I ever come acrost. It's a shed or somethink, and there was a car in it when I goes by. P'raps there was two. Loony!"

"What kind of a car was it?" asked the horsy individual. "One of those small run-abouts, what?"

"Small runabout nothink! It was a big car. Grey one; 'old six comfortable. They come upon me when I was pokin' around the car, see—door of the garridge was hopen— and that's wot Started 'em bein' cross."

"Oh, go and talk somewhere else," snapped the innkeeper, whose lack of company in that remote district seemed to have cured him of any appetite for it. "Let the gentleman drink 'is beer, and get along, do."

"I've finished my beer, thank you," drawled the horsy man, tossing a coin on the counter as he rose. "Good afternoon."

"Arternoon," murmured the innkeeper, folding his arms and sinking back comfortably in his chair behind the counter.

The tramp allowed the horsy man to go out first, and then slouched after him.

"Queer cove, ain't 'e?" said the pedlar. "They seems orl queer coves about these parts."

The horsy individual adjusted an eye-glass, the better to study his grimy companion. Then, suddenly making up his mind, he asked a question.

"I wonder if you could tell me the number of that motor-car?" he enquired.

"Wot? Think it's yourn?" grinned the ragamuffin. "I only re-members the larst two numbers, 'cos the plate seemed to 'ave got tucked away some'ow—so p'raps it *was* stolen, eh? The num-bers was 21, and I knows becos' it's the same as me age, I don't think!"

This information made a visible impression on the horsy in-dividual.

"I'll tell you something, my man," he said. "I have had a car stolen, and, do you know, your description just tallies with my car. I wonder—" He paused, as though hesitating. "Could you direct me to that cottage in the wood?"

The pedlar did so, and then added, in a serious voice: "But I wouldn't go there, sir." He looked around him, anxiously. "Look 'ere, sir. I ses to meself, 'There's somethink hup 'ere,' I ses. I ses to meself, it's fishy. The place is packed with people. When I ses packed, I don't mean like sardines, mind, but there's 'arf a dozen, easy, and they ain't up ter no good, that I'll swear to. I 'eard a scream onst, so I thinks—a young lidy's scream. And there's a tall gen'lman there—bit forin' lookin', grey 'air, my 'ight—cam't mistake 'im—well, sir, 'e's a devil, if there ever was one, so I ses. Ah, but if yer likes a pretty woman, p'raps it's worth riskin' the devil." He chuckled coarsely. Then he grew serious again. "But, jokin' apart, sir, if it's yer motor-car yer after, don't you go there alone, that's orl I ses. You git the perlice ter 'elp yer, see— and I reckon twelve won't be too many with that 'ouseful!"

"Thank you," said the horsy-looking individual. "You've done me a great service."

"Don't menshun," answered the tramp, and trudged away through the trees.

"By Jove!" murmured Wilfred Hobson, watching the pedlar go. "God bless that tramp!"

And, at the same moment, the tramp was murmuring: "God bless Wilfred Hobson!"

CHAPTER 11

Geoffrey Mordaunt, pedlar, kept on his way, without looking back, for ten minutes. Then he turned abruptly to the left, and increased his speed. The leisurely gait of a road-merchant was replaced by the swift walk of a man with a very definite purpose.

Presently a slight frown spread over his features. He had spied a figure among the trees, and the figure had spied him. The portly frame of Tobias King approached.

"I thought I'd come to look for you," observed Tobias, in his high treble. "Really, your disguise is remarkable—remarkable!"

"Much obliged, Tobias," replied Geoffrey, as they fell into pace. "My frame is some-what easier to disguise than your own, however."

"Alas, that is true," sighed Tobias. "Portliness has its disadvantages. Well, and how did you get on?"

"My scouting was quite satisfactory," said Geoffrey. "Not a suspicious sign anywhere."

"What about the innkeeper?" asked Tobias.

The tone was innocent, but slightly too innocent. Geoffrey gave a guarded reply.

"Why should one worry about the innkeeper?" he said.

"Quite so, quite so," conceded Tobias. "But it would be awkward if we ever had any trouble with him, eh?"

"Again, why should we have trouble?"

Tobias shrugged his shoulders. "One hears of traitors in camps," he remarked. "A bribe might tempt the innkeeper from his allegiance, you know. Such things have happened."

Geoffrey smiled. So the sleepy innkeeper was one of their own feather!

"I expect, if that innkeeper ever accepted such a bribe," he said, "he would wake up one morning to find himself dead. Eh, Tobias?"

"Ha, ha," chuckled Tobias. "It would be highly probable."

"Well, so much for my news. Now what of yours?" asked Geoffrey.

"Nothing. Excepting that girl. She's a bit of a nuisance."

"In what way?"

"She insists on an interview with you. That story I told her about her sweetheart still being alive—a silly story, perhaps, but I had to invent something to get her away from Littlehampton quickly—well, that story's got on her mind, and, even now, she is like the girl in Watt's picture, playing on the broken harp of hope. Although she knows the whole thing was a ruse, I seem to have awakened an idea in her mind, and it will be your job to dissipate it."

"What is her idea, exactly?" asked Geoffrey.

"Why, that your brother isn't dead, but confined in one of our sylvan Homes for Good and Annoying People."

"H'm. Well, I'll easily knock that idea on the head," muttered Geoffrey, wondering what would happen if he were to act upon his impulse to take out his revolver and shoot Tobias King. "She's being treated properly, of course?"

"Of course, my dear friend, of course. Have I not always agreed with your principle that brutality should never be tried until gentleness has failed? By the way, I suppose you think I did right to carry her off? Things are getting too warm for us, my beloved Chief, and it occurs to me that we shall soon have to flit in earnest. When we have—say— twenty thousand pounds, in the shape of a certain ruby, eh? Meanwhile, it is best to keep those who have most reason to do us mischief from doing said mischief." He raised his eyebrows. "You agree?"

"Oh yes, I suppose so. But we're raising too many hornets' nests. I'm not quite sure whether this was wise."

"My friend," said Tobias, solemnly, "I have kept a close watch on events lately. I always do. Though I may be in the background, I see many things. And I know that, if Miss Heather had remained at large, she would have thought of us, and dreamt of us, and harried us, and worried the lives out of us. She would have bought a revolver with one pretty little object—the object of shooting you. Believe me, I had some method in my madness."

"Well, let us leave Miss Heather for the moment. Have you any other news?"

"I have. Very interesting news. The police found the ruby where you divined it to be. The only fly in the ointment was that it didn't happen to be a ruby, after all, but a fake."

"Really? Is that so?" exclaimed Geoffrey Mordaunt.

"It is so. And I am wondering just how much this means. Baxter swears that he thought it was the genuine thing when it was passed on to him. Since we trust nobody, we must suspect Baxter of having substituted the imitation for the real. But I am inclined to think that, if there was any substitution, the delinquent was Joe. He knows plenty of people in the trade, and one pal in particular. Realizing that he was commissioned to steal the ruby, he may have had the imitation prepared in advance, and have kept the genuine stone while passing the sham one on to Baxter. It's only a theory, but worth considering."

"It's a very good theory," agreed Geoffrey. "But we'll search James Cardhew's house, just the same."

Tobias nodded, and they paced the last stretch to the cottage in silence.

Geoffrey would have given much for half an hour's solitude. His mind was working so fast, and his emotions were in such a tangle, that he longed for time to review himself and think matters out. But he was met at the door by Beatrice, who asked him to see Joan Heather at once and to get an inevitable interview over.

"Certainly," replied Geoffrey. "I will see her at once. Where is she?"

"In the sitting-room. We are making her comfortable. But she is very ungrateful." Beatrice smiled. "How she hates you, John!"

"It is hardly to be expected," muttered Geoffrey, "that she could love me. I had better see her alone."

He spoke on impulse. Perhaps, after all, he could find some way of disclosing himself without prejudicing his work; and, even if he did prejudice that work, had he any right to cause her such suffering? And then, against that thought, he realized that Joan's own safety depended entirely upon the preservation of his false relationship with her captors, and that the slightest slip might prove fatal. She herself, in her joy of discovering that Geoffrey was alive and by her side, might find it humanly impossible to keep her joy within her. A smile, a flicker, a gesture however slight, might betray the fact, and destroy, in an instant, the whole house of cards.

So he did not combat Tobias's bland suggestion that he would like to be present at the interview, and, when Beatrice raised her eyebrows, he shrugged his shoulders and nodded. She might as well be there, too.

He was relieved to find, on entering the room, that Joan was calm, although she was sadly pale, and her eyes burned with controlled anger and grief. She looked fully at Geoffrey Mordaunt for some while, and her steady, scornful gaze was one of the most trying ordeals he had ever gone through. At last she spoke, and he admired her for the steadiness of her voice.

"Will you answer me a few questions?" she asked. "I address them to you because I cannot get any satisfactory answers from the others, and because you seem to be the leader of this party of curs."

"I will answer your questions, if I can," replied Geoffrey, struggling with a feeling of suffocation. He wondered whether his fiancé was suffering more than he was? If so, he pitied her from the depths of his heart.

"First, why am I brought here?"

"I think you have been told that," said Geoffrey. "It is because circumstances have made you our avowed enemy, and we think you are less likely to harm us here than elsewhere.

"Your avowed enemy! Yes, that is true," she exclaimed, with bitterness. "How could it be otherwise?"

"We realize it could not be otherwise," observed Tobias, softly, "and that is the answer to your question. You are on the war-path, Miss Heather."

"I am so much on the war-path," she replied, "that, if ever I do get away from you, there is no stone I shall leave unturned to bring you all to justice."

"Those are brave words," said Geoffrey.

"Oh, I'm not afraid of you. Now, please, answer another question." She paused, and controlled herself with difficulty. "I want to know this. Is Geoffrey Mordaunt really dead? Or are you keeping him somewhere— as you are keeping me?"

Geoffrey felt Tobias's eyes upon him, and dared not hesitate.

"Geoffrey Mordaunt was too dangerous a man to take any chances with," he replied, and turned his eyes away because he could not bear to see her hopes dashed so cruelly to the ground.

"He is dead then?" she whispered. "Really dead? You swear it?"

Geoffrey shrugged his shoulders, and tried to believe that the whole thing was a bad dream.

"Say it—say it!" she insisted, looking him full in the face.

"He is dead."

"By whose hand?"

"Mine!"

Suddenly she darted forward, and struck him on his cheek. "Now kill me, too!" she cried, and sank down weakly at his feet.

He bent down, and lifted her up gently. She hung heavy in his arms, and he knew that she had fainted. He carried her to the sofa, and, as he placed her upon it, allowed his cheek to touch hers for an instant, as though by accident. More, he dared not do. He feared, indeed, that he had done too much, and forced harshness into his voice when next he spoke.

"See to her, Beatrice," he said, thickly. "We can't waste more time over such scenes. When she comes to, put her in a bedroom, and see that she is not disturbed. Lock her in, and bring me the key."

He turned and left them, and, in order to afford some apparent pretext for his abrupt departure, strode along the passage till he came to Jones's room. Unlocking the door, he went in.

"Well, Jones," he said, as the pale young man looked up, "have you done any thinking?"

"I have," replied Jones.

"And what have you decided?"

"I've decided to come in with you."

"Sensible fellow. You'll do better with us than on your own, and we want people like you." He stepped out into the passage, and called, "Tobias! Baxter!" And, when they appeared, he told them of Jones's decision.

"Capital, capital," purred Tobias. "We've some gaps that need filling."

"And there will be more gaps, I hope," thought Geoffrey, "before the evening's out." Aloud he said: "Have a chat with him, you two, and initiate him as far as is necessary."

"Won't you stay and join in the chat?" asked Tobias.

"No, not now. I have some chatting I want to do with Beatrice."

"I wonder," said Tobias, benignly, "whether I shall ever wholly and absolutely trust you, John?"

"Why worry about it, Tobias," smiled Geoffrey back, "when we get along so famously on a basis of mutual suspicion?"

He heard Tobias's chuckle as he turned his back and made his way to the sitting-room.

Soon, Beatrice joined him. All the minor details of his scheme were working smoothly, and with clockwork rapidity. As he had anticipated, there was a gleam of jealousy in Beatrice's eye as she held out the key to Joan's room.

"I have followed out your instructions to the letter," she said. "Miss Heather is, for the moment, quite safe."

"What should I care for her safety?" demanded Geoffrey.

"Oh, how do I know?" she retorted, with affected carelessness. "Don't ask me!"

"I do ask you. You are behaving like a silly, jealous child." She would have interrupted him angrily, but he went on, "I asked just now, 'What do I care for her safety?' Well, that was wrong. I do care—and so do you. If dead men tell no tales, they play havoc with the ranks of such people as us, and that is a point which might not be fully realized by the other inmates of this house. What's got to be done will be done. I didn't hesitate to kill my brother the other day, did I? Very well, then. Be satisfied that, when a moment is ripe, I strike—and the girl upstairs will prove no exception to my rule."

"Is that why you insist on keeping the key of the room yourself?" asked Beatrice.

"You're a fool, Beatrice," he answered. "Our position is delicate enough as it is, and I do not intend to make it more so by unwise roughness—that's all. But, in order to prove to you that you're on quite a wrong track, I'll hand this key to Mrs Jowl and you and I will take a little walk."

She looked at him curiously. "What kind of a walk?" she enquired. "A business one or a sentimental one?"

"Put on your hat," he replied, "and you'll find out."

She hesitated, then left the room to obey. The next moment, Geoffrey was in the kitchen, where Mrs Jowl was bending over the fire. She looked up as he approached.

"Now, listen to me, Mrs, Jowl," said Geoffrey, in a low voice. "I want you to take charge of the key to Miss Heather's room, and you are not to give it up to anyone excepting myself—you understand?—or the police—"

"The police!" gasped Mrs Jowl.

"Tsch! Don't be a fool, woman! It isn't likely that the police will trouble us, but one never knows, and what I'm telling you is for your own good. If we *are* caught here, the police will thank anyone who leads them to Miss Heather, and who has treated her well. You could say that you were sorry for her, and had seen that no harm came to her. But, after all, that's hardly here or there, for, when Miss Fullerton and I come back from our walk. I'll have that key back again. In my absence, I am favouring you because you've served me well and I can trust you. You understand?"

"Yes, sir," replied Mrs Jowl, flattered. "No one shan't touch the key but me."

He nodded, and returned to the passage. Beatrice had just descended, and they walked out into the woods together.

"Where are we going?" asked Beatrice.

He answered her by asking a question himself.

"Do you know these woods intimately?" he said.

"No, I don't. They'd take some knowing, I should think"

"My view, exactly. If we're tracked, we shall be caught like rats in a trap."

"But why should we be tracked?" she demanded.

"I hope we won't be, my dear." He noted her pleasure at the appellation. "All the same, I never leave more to chance than is necessary, and it's impossible to ignore the fact that the net is closing around us. Every day, we make more enemies, and lose more friends. You've seen that."

"Yes, I have, John," she replied, "and— I can't make it out. Things seem to have been going wrong ever since that day you killed your brother." ("How coolly," thought Geoffrey, "she talks of it!") Can *you* explain it?"

Geoffrey fought a sudden impulse to laugh. Could he explain it? He pictured her face had he given the true explanation. Instead, however, he gave her a plausible alternative.

"Oh, I think it's easily explained," he said. "Things move in cycles, you know. We are passing through a bad phase—a phase of nerves and jumps and unwise decisions. Nothing is so unbalancing as jealousy, Beatrice. It has brought James Cardhew low. Maybe it will bring others."

"Oh! So you think that's the reason?"

"One reason, yes. Another is that Geoffrey Mordaunt's death has awakened fresh activity at Scotland Yard, fresh desires to capture us. That's natural, isn't it? And so, because of that, you and I are walking through these woods to become a little more conversant with them—to find, perhaps, a route that might be followed by us if we're cornered."

"I can't help thinking, John," said Beatrice, after a short pause, as they wound their way through the thick trees, "that you have some other reason up your sleeve?"

"Yes, I have another reason," he admitted. "The future looks hazy. That ruby still tempts me. I want to think. It's impossible, cooped up in the cottage there."

"Two reasons, John," she murmured.

"And now for the third?"

"Is there a third?"

She shrugged her shoulders, and laughed. They walked on for awhile in silence.

Ahead of them, through a gap in the trees, a sheet of water glowed in the early evening sunlight. At each end, the trees thickened and became impenetrable, so that one had either to swerve to right or left for a path, unless there were a route across the lake. Reaching the water's edge, Geoffrey stopped and scanned the rushes.

"What are you looking for?" asked Beatrice. "A boat?"

Geoffrey nodded, and then pointed to an old punt, rotting among the reeds. It looked as though it would fall to pieces when touched.

"No, thank you," commented Beatrice. "Let's turn back."

"We might try it?" suggested Geoffrey.

"Why should we try it? I have no desire to risk drowning. Your mood isn't in the least entertaining, John." She glanced at him impatiently. "Come along—let's go back. I'm tired of this."

Geoffrey took no notice of her. He was already approaching the boat.

"Are you coming?" she repeated, annoyed.

"No, Beatrice, I am not. I'm going to see whether this boat is workable."

"Then I shall return alone."

He looked at her suddenly. Three voices cried into his ear. The first said, "Let her go back, and be caught." The second said, "Keep her with you—she is useful." And the third, louder than the rest, cried, "Keep her with you—she is, after all, a woman."

While he hesitated, she turned, and began walking away. But suddenly she stopped, and lifted her head. A shot echoed in the distance.

Geoffrey heard himself swearing horribly and realistically. The part of John was second nature to him now. He called to Beatrice, and she came hurrying back to him.

"Damn them!" he cried. "They *have* hunted us down, after all. I reckon it's a case of *sauve qui peut!*"

"Yes, we'll have to risk the boat, after all," replied Beatrice, and held out her arms, that he might help her into it.

For an instant they touched, and in that instant she pressed herself close to him. A twig had cracked close by.

"Get your revolver handy, John," she whispered. "As you say, it's *sauve qui peut.*"

Her voice was steady, but he felt the slight tremor of her body, and it rejoiced him to realize that even such a woman as Beatrice Fullerton could fear.

Then a figure plunged towards them through the trees. Had it been one of his own gang, he would have shot without scruple, telling Beatrice afterwards that he had not realized it till too late. But the figure was unfamiliar, and Geoffrey's revolver wavered. To risk his own life in this enterprise was one thing. To shoot a fellow-detective in cold blood was another. Yet, if he did not shoot, it was the end.

"Shoot—shoot!" cried Beatrice. "Why do you hesitate?"

"Because he can see through a borrowed hat and coat," replied the new-comer, in a high treble.

And the next moment Geoffrey found himself being bored searchingly by the eyes of Tobias King.

CHAPTER 12

Wilfred Hobson, after leaving the communicative tinker, did not waste any time. He returned full speed to Brackleton, and the owner of the hired bicycle he rode would have looked anxious could he have seen how recklessly his customer was driving it over the ruts and furrows. He might have charged something for depreciation of tyres.

Yet even he would have come round to the view that there were extenuating circumstances had he known all there was to know, and had he realized that the next destination of his customer, after delivering back the machine, was the local police station. But the cycle dealer was not an enterprising man, and a bothersome puncture was on his mind.

Two minutes later, the local police-station was in a ferment. Hurried orders were being given, 'phone wires became busy, and indolent officials suddenly stopped yawning and grew keen and alert. In a very short while, Wilfred Hobson was retracing his way back through the woods, accompanied this time by a score of companions who, if they differed in skill, were united by a common purpose and a common zest.

In thinking afterwards over the events of the next half-hour Wilfred found that his usually clear mind was somewhat incoherent. It was as though a great force of uncontrolled man-power had been suddenly released against an unknown, untested factor, and the unreality of the business was enhanced by the thick, dreamy wood in which the events took place. There had been no time for a settled plan of campaign, worked out in thorough detail. There had been no time to collect the exact kind of man-power required. Therefore Wilfred Hobson had gathered unto himself quantity rather than quality. The whole thing was bewildering, rapid guesswork.

And the man-power released itself of its own accord, without waiting for orders. This was because the greater half of it was undisciplined. The sight of the cottage had whetted the invaders' appetites, and the sudden appearance of a frightened figure had done the rest. Four or five of the company dashed towards the figure. The figure fled, tripped, and fell. And so the bonds were loosed, and confusion began its reign.

Wilfred and three or four officials alone kept their heads. While two of their worthy helpers were fighting and trying to arrest each other, they entered the cottage by the back entrance, and, with revolvers ready, toured the place. There was never any question of parley. The inmates acted immediately like trapped rats, seeking impossible escapes, and proclaiming their guilt by their attitude.

Jowl put up the biggest fight. He had the strength of three men, and it took just three to overpower him. While that was being done, Wilfred was struggling with a locked door, and calling for assistance to bash it in.

A stout man, in official uniform, ran up to him,

"Here's the key," he cried. "Got it off the old woman. I'll call the boys inside."

He dashed out again, while Hobson slipped the key into the lock. As he opened the door, he heard the stout official bawling:

"Come along in, boys—we're wanted!"

There was a rush for the cottage. The stout official, however, went out to scour the woods, and did not return. It was not he, but another official, who was found a few minutes later under a bush, wounded, and without his cap and coat.

Hobson swung the door inwards, and a cry escaped him. Joan Heather, with wide, terror-stricken eyes, was sitting on a bed, staring at him.

"Thank God!" murmured the young man, fervently, and hurried forward to reassure her.

"Mr Hobson!" she gasped.

"Miss Heather!" he replied, flushed with joy and exertion. "Thank heaven you're safe!"

There was a moment's silence, while eyes regarded her curiously from the passage. Then she asked, faintly:

"Are they all caught?"

"I believe so," answered Wilfred Hobson. "We'll have a count."

A sudden commotion outside caused him to dash out again. One of the prisoners had escaped. A frenzied figure sped through the trees, but he did not speed for long. A young policeman, racing after him, suddenly stopped, raised his revolver, and made the best shot of his career. Baxter's account was paid at last.

"Sorry, sir," said the policeman, returning, falsely apologetic, for he was bursting with pride. "'Ad to do it."

Wilfred nodded.

"You did quite right," he said, quietly. "We don't want more bloodshed than is necessary, but this gang's too dangerous to allow any escapes. And now let us see who we've got."

The prisoners were trotted forward. Wilfred was disappointed at their number. There were only three—a large man, with a sandy beard and huge, handcuffed hands, a sullen, scowling young fellow, and a frightened old woman, who chattered and mumbled about a key she had given up, and her hope that this kindly act would bring her consideration. The body of Baxter, in the wood, made the fourth capture.

A pang of disappointment shot through Wilfred Hobson, and for an instant he lost his usual coolness.

"Why are you all in here?" he shouted, angrily. "There are more to be caught yet!"

"We were told to come," said somebody.

Wilfred nodded. His anger passed, though the disappointment remained.

"So you were," he said. "I remember hearing it. Where's the man who gave the order?" No one came forward. "Well—who was it? It was a stout man—the man who gave me the key to this door. Where is he?"

"Ah, the wretch!" cried the old woman, shaking her bony fist!

"That was Mr King! He snatched the key from me—but I was going to give it to you, anyhow, so I was!" Her voice became wheedling again. "I wouldn't let 'em hurt the poor girl." She spat. "Bad luck to 'im!"

Wilfred bit his lip, and turned to Joan.

"Wasn't it a stout man—this Mr King—who brought you here. Miss Heather?" he asked.

"Yes. A man with a high voice."

"That's the fellow. And what about—the arch-fiend? Was he here, too?" Joan nodded. "Then we've lost the two most slippery customers in the kingdom Well, come along. Spread around, boys. We'll have them yet."

"There was also the woman," said Joan. "She must have got away with them. It was she who locked me in here shortly before you came."

"By Jove!" cried Hobson. "What a wealth of criminality this forest contains!"

"Not to mention places to 'ide 'em in," added a constable.

Fresh plans were hurriedly made, but many predicted failure before the search began. The wood, in places, was almost impenetrable, and there was no indication as to whether to search north, south, east or west. The discovery of the wounded official caused some delay. Then, those who could be spared set out in small groups to scour the difficult land.

Wilfred Hobson took one man with him, the young constable who had shot Baxter, and he chose a direction contrary to that suggested by the position of the wounded man under the bush. He divined, correctly, that a man of Tobias King's subtlety would very likely have moved the unconscious form for the very purpose of setting the pursuers on a wrong track. It was the position of the body, in fact, that had determined the direction of most of the searchers. Wilfred and his constable took an exactly opposite course.

They made their way with as much speed as was compatible with thoroughness and caution, searching likely and unlikely places as they went. For awhile nothing rewarded them. The young constable began to grow gloomy amid the lonely, depressing surroundings, and found himself dwelling upon a comfortable inn, where the lamps would soon be lit, and congenial company would foregather. He shuddered as he contemplated the possibility of being caught by the night in this tall, tangled, trackless forest.

Still, he kept his eyes skinned, and Hobson was able to make a subsequent report which assisted him towards his cherished promotion.

Presently they came to a spot where the bushes appeared to have been recently broken through. And, a little later, an exclamation from the constable brought Hobson quickly to his side.

"Look at this, six," said the constable, holding up a tiny scrap of dark blue material, "Lady passed this way, looks like it."

Hobson examined the piece of stuff, nodded, and put it in his pocket.

"Yes, we're on the right track, without much doubt," he exclaimed. "I wish we had a few more hours of daylight, though."

"Ah," agreed the constable, "so do I!"

But their hopes had revived, and they continued their search with renewed care and watchfulness. A sheet of water opened before them. They scanned its surface eagerly, but it revealed nothing. At either end of the water the forest had gathered itself as though to make an impassable barrier. They stopped and considered.

"I suppose one can get round?" queried Hobson, doubtfully.

"I reckon it'd take us a good few miles," replied the constable, "and it's none too light, sir. What do you think?"

"Perhaps there's a boat?"

"P'raps."

They began to search among the rushes, and, this time, it was Hobson who gave the cry.

"Look here!" he exclaimed, pointing to an empty space, where the reeds were bent and crushed. "What do you make of that?"

The constable nodded gloomily. His prospects of a night in the wood were substantially increasing.

"Yes, sir," he said. "There's been a boat there. And it's only been took out recent."

"Then—they've crossed."

"Yes, sir."

"We'll have to do the same."

The constable made no reply. Hobson looked at him, and smiled. He was quite in sympathy with the constable. Nevertheless, duty came before pleasure.

"Can you swim? "he asked.

"Yes, sir," replied the constable, in a depressed voice.

"Well, I'm going to swim across to the other side. Will you come with me?"

"I'm taking my orders from you, sir."

"I don't insist."

"Thank you, sir. I'll come."

He was already preparing himself, and Hobson gave a grunt of satisfaction. They wrapped up their revolvers as best they could, and waded in. The slime near the shore worried them at first, but they soon found deep water, and struck out for the opposite shore, about half a mile distant. The water was clear and cold.

Half-way across, Hobson suddenly cried out:

"There's a strong current here. Keep to the left."

The constable obeyed, while Hobson struck towards the left himself. Evidently there was a fall of water at the right-hand end of the lake, and he had been too close to it. By altering their course they evaded it, and were soon floundering out on the opposite shore.

Here they found the trees slightly thinner, and they were able to go round to the end of the water where the fall was. It was, to their surprise, quite a substantial one, tumbling over big boulders and rocks beneath an almost impenetrable archway of tangled green. They were about to turn away when a large portion of broken wood disengaged itself from between two rocks in which it had become wedged, staggered into the stream, and was swept downwards, to break on another jagged rock lower down.

"By Jove," exclaimed Hobson. "Did you see that?"

"Yes, sir," replied the constable, solemnly. "Bit of a boat."

They looked at each other, and silently retraced their steps to the spot where they had landed. Walking on a hundred yards through the wood they suddenly saw a figure not far off. It was the figure of a man, and the man stared at them for a moment, and then turned away leisurely and disappeared.

"Come along," cried Hobson, hurrying forward. "We must interview that chap. If he's seen nothing of the people we're after—well, I imagine they must have taken the same course as that bit of broken boat."

When they reached the spot where the man had stood, they saw him in a little clearing a short way off, standing by a wood pile. Near him, also, was a small cart, with a patient pony. The man was obviously a wood-cutter, and the cart was half-stacked.

"Hi!" shouted Hobson, hailing the man. "Have you seen any people pass this way?"

The wood-cutter shook his head.

"No, sir, I ain't," he replied.

"Are you sure?"

"Course I'm sure! I'd 'a knowd if I'd 'a seed 'em."

"Well, have you heard anything?"

"No, I ain't 'eard nothing, neither. All I seed was a boat cornin' across the water."

"Ah! When was that?"

The wood-cutter scratched his thick head. "Mebbe twenty minutes—I can't say. I called to 'em not to go too close to the current. It's dangerous. Ah, mebbe you was with the party. I sees you're wet."

"We were not with the party, my man. We're looking for the party. Do you suppose, as they don't seem to have landed here, they *did* go too near the current?"

"I tell you, I don't know," retorted the man. "Mebbe they went back. I mus' get on wi' my work."

Hobson considered a moment. Then he said:

"We're looking for three dangerous criminals. They're wanted for the worst sort of crime, including murder. If you're hiding anything—"

"What should I 'ide?" exclaimed the wood-cutter, indignantly. "Why shouldn't I tell yer if I'd seed anything?"

"All right. Don't get excited. Where do you live?"

"Cottage up the road."

"How far?"

"Mile."

"Anybody there now?"

"Yes—my old woman."

"Well, I'm thinking someone had better go and see that she comes to no harm. I advise you to get along home—"

"I can't till I've finished this work. We've lived in the woods all our lives. We ain't afeared."

"Perhaps not. But suppose these rascals have slipped by you, and are taking refuge in your cottage?"

"Bah!" said the wood-cutter. "Old woman's tales."

"I think we ought to search the cottage, and make sure everything's all right, sir," suggested the constable.

"So do I," agreed Hobson. "We'll go there right away. If we find nothing, we'll come back and have a look for the bodies. I imagine our friends have gone to their last reckoning." He turned to the wood-cutter. "Coming along with us?"

"No," answered the wood-cutter, resuming his chopping. "I've got to fill my cart. You don't want me."

"Well, if we find anything wrong with your wife," said Hobson, motioning the constable to start, "I'll have you charged with neglect."

The only reply vouchsafed was an expectoration. They heard the woodman's axe chopping away as they departed.

"Keep it up," commanded a low voice from a clump of bushes, "or you'll get a bullet."

The wood-chopper kept it up. He worked steadily, without

pause, till approaching footsteps announced the return of Hobson and the constable. They nodded as they passed him.

"All safe," reported Hobson. "I don't imagine you'll be troubled. But it's a lonely spot. Would you like someone to spend the night with you?"

"No," answered the woodman. "Why should I?"

"Well, if I weren't pretty certain that my friends are no longer in the land of the living, I should insist on it. Report anything you come across or hear to the nearest police station. Good night."

They trudged away. Soon, the trees and the gathering dusk swallowed them up. The woodman hesitated.

"Go on," said the voice from the bushes.

With a muttered oath, he fell to his chopping again, till another command came. This time, he was told to go and look at the lake. He went off obediently, and a stout figure emerged from the bushes as he did so, keeping some way behind him, and ever covering him with his revolver. Presently the wood-cutter returned, and reported that two heads were bobbing in the water, making for the opposite shore.

"And what next?" asked the wood-cutter. "I'll expect to be paid for this."

"You are being paid, my friend," replied Tobias King, sweetly. "We are paying you by presenting you with your life."

"You promised me more than that," retorted the woodman.

"You shall receive more than that," answered another voice, as Geoffrey Mordaunt, assisted by Beatrice, also emerged from the bushes. He was limping. "Provided you continue to obey us, you'll not be forgotten. But the moment you attempt to play us false—" He tapped his revolver.

"Oh, I'll not play any monkey tricks," said the woodman. "I know which side my bread's buttered. What am I to do now?"

"You will stop chopping wood, give me a seat in your cart, and conduct us to your cottage."

"Won't that be rather awkward?" asked the man, doubtfully.

"Not half so awkward, I assure you, as it will be if you refuse.

I have no doubt your wife will be ready to take your point of view, when you explain it to her. We shall stay the night."

"A bit risky," muttered the wood-cutter.

"Not at all," answered Geoffrey. "Your cottage has been searched. You won't be troubled again. And, in the morning, we shall leave you—and also a five-pound note."

"Very well," said the man, his eye gleaming. "Beggars can't be choosers."

Beatrice helped Geoffrey on to the cart, and the mile trudge through the trees began.

It was a strange procession. The pony alone saw nothing unusual in it. The wood-cutter was wondering whether it was to prove a lucky or unlucky day for him. Tobias, usually placid and urbane, did his best to conceal his scowls. Geoffrey, thinking hard, kept one eye on Tobias. And Beatrice kept her eyes on both of them.

Matters, Geoffrey reflected, were reaching a psychological climax. There had been no time yet for explanations between him and Tobias, but he was conscious that a very definite change had come into their relationship, and he was longing for an opportunity to review it, and, if necessary, to readjust it. The boat had proved every bit as frail as it had looked. Water had flowed freely into its rotting boards, and it had drifted, a sodden mass, towards the dangerous current and the falls. It was only by the greatest effort and the narrowest chance that they had evaded a catastrophe, and had managed to steer the boat so that its inevitable course was delayed by an impact with a rock. Beatrice had jumped free, Tobias had followed, and Geoffrey felt certain that Tobias had done his best, in the scramble, to prevent him from following likewise. The detective placed responsibility for his barked knee entirely on Tobias King.

Darkness was now falling rapidly. As they neared the cottage, the woodman ran on ahead to prepare his wife for the arrival, and it was a very pale old woman who stood at the door to welcome them. Geoffrey, touched by her pathetic face, hastened to reassure her that she need fear no harm, and that she would find them profitable guests. Then he demanded a sofa and a bowl of water; and, two minutes later, Beatrice knelt beside him and attended to his hurt.

He rolled his trousers up to his knee, in order that she might bathe the wound. It was not a bad wound, but she gave a gasp before she applied the sponge. Geoffrey looked at her enquiringly.

"What's the matter?" he asked.

"Nothing," she answered, regaining her composure as suddenly as she had lost it.

But there was a curious glint in her eye which Geoffrey tried in vain to fathom.

CHAPTER 13

"In half an hour," said Tobias to Beatrice, musingly, "our dear John will have finished his sleep—he is ever punctual—and will join us in conference. There will be grave things to discuss, my child. Very grave things," His small eyes closed, in contemplation of their gravity. "And it occurs to me that, in the meantime, you and I might do well to tell each other what we are thinking."

Beatrice looked at her companion thoughtfully. They had the sitting-room to themselves. Upstairs, in one of the two bedrooms which the cottage boasted, the wood-cutter and his wife were sleeping the sleep of the more or less just, while, in the other bedroom, Geoffrey Mordaunt was taking a short, much needed rest.

"I'm quite willing to hear your thoughts," replied Beatrice, after a pause, "and to pay a penny for them. But perhaps mine aren't worth so much."

"You underrate your value," observed Tobias. "And, perhaps, mine as well. But, be that as it may, you shall have my thoughts for nothing. Our friendship is beyond L.S.D., eh?"

"On the contrary," returned Beatrice, "our friendship is bound up in nothing else."

"Perhaps you are right. Then I will substitute 'common interest' for 'friendship'"—He paused. "No, no, Beatrice, I refuse to place our association on so low a rung. I have a great admiration for you, my child, a great admiration. There is, in fact, only one thing I would not do for you, and that is, harm myself." He chuckled. "Apart from that single exception, I am ever your adoring slave."

"If these are the thoughts you value at over a penny," she re-

118

marked, "they are disappointing."

Tobias was not in the least abashed. He had patience and poise. For three years he had wanted Beatrice, and he would wait another three years, if necessary. Or he would strike at once, if necessary. Delay was not a principle with him; he merely realized its inestimable value in difficult and delicate situations, and his eagerness to attain his ends was to be measured by his refusal to weaken himself by breathless rushing. It would have been easy and desirable to take Beatrice in his arms at this moment. But, in the end, it would have removed her farther from him. So he smiled, and schooled his impulses.

"Very well, then," he said, nodding amiably, "I will give you some thoughts that are really worth quite a penny. Here is one. Quite a simple little thought, but none the less arresting. What bad luck we have been having lately."

"We have," admitted Beatrice. "What of it?"

"What of it? Exactly, my dear child. What of it? Well, I think quite a lot of it So much, in fact, that I would like to run over the recent course of events with you. You recall, doubtless, a certain ruby?"

"We all have reason to."

"You recall its worth—some twenty thousand pounds. You recall our comparative poverty. To what, by the way, do you ascribe our comparative poverty?"

"We've made some big hauls lately," said Beatrice, reflectively. "Nothing like twenty thousand pounds, but things haven't been so bad—"

"And yet we feel the pinch?"

"Yes. Money has flowed in, but it's also flowed out again."

"Ah, my beautiful Beatrice, I knew I should not be disappointed in you," exclaimed Tobias. "We are getting to the root cause. Go on with your logic."

She looked at him, and smiled. On the whole, she found this analysis rather entertaining.

"Well, Tobias, the reason why the money has flowed out is because the expenses have been heavy."

"And the reason why expenses have been heavy is because there have been too many people to pay. You see the drift?"

"I think so. But I daresay you can make it plainer."

"I can. Now, listen. To gain that ruby would make many things possible. It might even allow some of us to become temporarily respectable again, until necessity or boredom drove us back to the secluded life. But, had we gained that ruby—well, say, a week ago, quite a number of people would have wanted a bite of it who are now—alas!—on the verge of biting nothing more edifying than prison bread. Run over this list with me. Joe Flipp. Edward Tapley. Baxter. Jowl. Mrs Jowl. Jones—but not, you note, John—"

"Or Beatrice or Tobias," interposed Beat-rice.

"Or Beatrice or Tobias—yet." He paused, closed his eyes, and put his head on one side. With his eyes still closed, he added, "But Tobias was very nearly added to that list this afternoon. Very nearly. The only person who saved Tobias from catastrophe was—Tobias."

He opened his eyes suddenly, and looked at her hard. She answered his look unflinchingly.

"You know me pretty well, Tobias," she said, coolly. "I don't think it is even in your mind that I have had anything to do with our failures."

"Right!" he purred, slapping his knee softly. "Quite and ever right, my child. I do not suspect you in the least. I do not even suggest that it was *your* suggestion that you and our beloved John should take a long stroll at a convenient time before the police raided the Jowls' cottage. But that stroll was rather interesting, was it not? The thought of it is worth every farthing of a penny? Don't you think so?"

Beatrice frowned slightly.

"I asked him what the idea was," she said, "and he told me that he wished to find some route of escape, in case the police did raid the place."

"Ah! Then he had it in his mind!"

"That's the first really foolish thing you've said," she retorted.

"Of course he had it in his mind. He always has had it in his mind, and, if he had not, both you and I would be eating prison bread at this moment, as well as all the other crowd."

"True," murmured Tobias, justly. "We owe him something."

"Of course we do. And that's why we must go slow in all this, Tobias. There may be something in what you say, but it all needs careful thinking over. Another reason he gave me for that walk was his need to think out a scheme to get hold of the ruby."

"And, of course—I make no imputation—he needed you for that?"

"John needs me in more ways that you imagine!" she shot back. "I am often with him when he is working out his schemes. But I am not going to suggest," she added, "that we think entirely of business when we are together."

Tobias nodded. He would like her to have suggested it. Nevertheless, he was sufficiently shrewd, and sufficiently above jealousy, to realize that Beatrice had betrayed more necessity for John's company than John had ever betrayed for hers.

"Well, let's get to roots," she said, suddenly. "What, exactly, is at the bottom of this discussion?"

"Nothing that should not be apparent from the top," he replied. "I assure you, I have no possible objection to this cutting down process—if such a process is in operation. I think, in principle, it is excellent. Quite worthy of the master mind. My sole anxiety is that both you and I shall remain among the immune ones. It is natural that I—that we—should not desire to be added to that list!"

"I don't feel any danger," replied Beatrice.

"No, you have little cause to. And perhaps, if I had been asked to accompany you on the sylvan stroll, I might have felt a similar optimism. Well, my dear, I think we have talked enough. There is no more to be said. But I invite you, my child, to bear in mind all I have said, to keep your eyes open, and, above all, to remember that Tobias King is your friend, to the gates of Hell and right into the warmth beyond, as long as you remain his."

Whereupon he folded his hands across his ample chest, and

closed his patient eyes. But Tobias King had the uncanny faculty of seeing through his lids, and he noted that Beatrice was frowning rather heavily.

CHAPTER 14

When Geoffrey Mordaunt entered the little sitting-room, he found two dozing inmates, but they awoke very quickly after his entrance and responded, with that instinct born of long training, to the necessities of the moment. Geoffrey himself, having slept soundly and awakened at the exact moment he had set his mind on, was full of fresh vigour.

"How is your leg?" asked Beatrice.

"Mending rapidly," he replied. "There's no need to think about it. It was quite a temporary wrench—for which I've not had time yet to thank you properly, Tobias," he said to that worthy. "If you hadn't been so wrapt up in your own safety when you got on that boulder there'd have been a little more room for me."

"On the brink of death," smiled Tobias, "we are not always Christian."

"It is only on the brink of death." retorted Geoffrey, "that some of us think of turning Christian."

"Our friend has slept well, Beatrice," beamed Tobias. "Note his wit. Ah, had we enjoyed your bed instead of these lumpy chairs, we might have been up to you."

"Well, there will be plenty of time to put that to the test," said Geoffrey. "After our chat, Beatrice can have the bed—which, let me say, has lumps of its own—and you, Tobias, may sleep there during the whole of tomorrow, if you wish."

"Oh, then you think we shall be staying here the whole of tomorrow?"

"I have quite decided, in my own mind, that it will be the best plan. There is bound to be a hue and cry after us, if the theory of our drowning doesn't gain acceptance—and our bodies will not be found, for obvious reasons. In that case, we ought to lie low until things have settled down a bit. The fact that this cottage has already been searched, and that our host has promised to report anything he comes across, will be on our side."

"Personally, I think the police are very likely to pay us another visit," observed Tobias.

"They may. That I admit. But it is simply a question of taking the lesser risk, and, if we are seen in any of the small villages or towns about here, our capture is certain. In a week, our chance will be better—or we may have devised a better plan."

"A week!" murmured Tobias, in a pained voice "It will be boring."

"I understand," said Geoffrey, dryly, "that solitary confinement is even more boring. Don't forget we are between the Devil and the deep sea."

Tobias nodded. For all his suspicions, he was forced to agree with his Chief's logic.

"Very well," he observed. "If Beatrice agrees, I am willing to submit to this preferable form of confinement—though, whether we are choosing the Devil or the deep sea, I am hazy."

"I agree, too," interposed Beatrice. "To discard our present shelter, until we find a better, would be madness."

"Good," said Geoffrey. "Then that is settled. For the time being we stay here. And our host will have to spy for us. Should the worst come to the worst, we may be able to escape in his cart, under a wood pile. Otherwise—well, we all have revolvers, and know how to use them."

"Do you trust our host upstairs?" queried Tobias.

"I believe that his moral code is wrapt up in his bank balance, like the rest of us," answered Geoffrey.

"Then you don't trust him?"

"Whether he is trustworthy or not will depend on just how we treat him. If need be, we must not hesitate to threaten him, or to give him pound-notes. As our stay will not be for eternity, I am inclined to think the pound-note treatment will suit us best. He is saving up, I have found out, to buy this cottage."

124

"What queer tastes some people have," commented Tobias.

Then the party broke up. Beatrice went up to the spare bedroom, while the two men settled themselves to conclude the night as comfortably as they could below.

In the middle of a deep sleep, Geoffrey opened his eyes suddenly to find a figure standing over him. It was Tobias, and it was characteristic of each man that neither showed the least sign of being flustered.

"What's the matter?" asked Geoffrey, in a sleepy, natural voice.

"I dreamt that you betrayed me," answered Tobias, "and it was so realistic that I had to come and reproach you."

"You don't trust me even in your dreams," smiled Geoffrey, closing his eyes again. "Tobias, I should have thought you were the last person to be afflicted with nerves."

"We were in a burning house," proceeded Tobias, "and you and Beatrice walked off, leaving me inside to burn."

"Which is practically what happened at the cottage when the police arrived," said Geoffrey, with eyes still closed. "Only we didn't walk off quite like that."

"Didn't you?"

Geoffrey opened his eyes, and studied his companion.

"I am more patient with you, Tobias, than with anybody else in the world," he said, at last, "and I accept more from you. Is it beside the argument to tell you that, if I really wanted to get rid of you, I have a revolver behind my cushion that would have made the task very simple?"

"There is no revolver behind your cushion," answered Tobias, blandly, "for I removed it before you woke up."

"Very pretty, Tobias. The only regret is that I hate to see real genius wasted. By the way, I don't suppose you really want to earn my enmity, Tobias, do you?"

"I wouldn't mind in the least," retorted Tobias, "if the battle were only between you and me—and, shall we say, Beatrice? But my battle is also against the world, and in *that* battle, dear John, you have proved yourself my superior. So I pin my faith to your flag, so long as you fight for me in that battle, and return you your revolver."

"Keep it till the morning," yawned Geoffrey Mordaunt, "if it will comfort you."

Tobias returned to his chair smiling, but with an annoying sense that he had not won. He retained the revolver, and would have given much to know whether his companion assigned his safety to an undisturbed relationship or to the exceeding riskiness of the sound of a shot on this still and menacing night?

He slept fitfully, an unusual thing for him, and, when morning dawned, and Beatrice descended from the poky room upstairs, he did not hesitate to take her place.

"Look at that brute snoring among those lumps!" he murmured to Beatrice, in aggrieved accents. "Sleep is largely a question of shape. Perfect rotundity requires the smoothest bed that can be found."

She assured him that he would find no smoothness upstairs; but he assured her, with equal certainty, that anything would appear smooth to him after the vacated arm-chair.

"I shall probably sleep till four," he added. "Do not wake me unless the handcuffs are actually at the door." And he ambled upstairs.

The day passed quietly, the tension decreasing as each hour slipped by. The anxious old lady, putting her trust in God and her hope in her guests' purses, tended and cooked for them, while the wood-cutter continued with his work in the woods and combined it with the most profitable scouting he had ever done in his life. A pound a day was his pay, on top of the original five pounds, which had materialized. Why, it was better than one got for the same job in the army!

He staved off one enquiry—and it was the only enquiry that came to his part of the woods. To have searched the woods thoroughly, with its hundreds of hiding places, would have been next to impossible, and by degrees the police grew more and more half-hearted in their activities. At last the search was temporarily abandoned, some accepting the theory that, although the bodies had not been found, the fugitives had met a watery fate, while others followed up clues farther afield.

Meanwhile, the fugitives themselves kept indoors, following a queer, confined regime. Tobias slept most of the time, excusing himself on the score that he had much lost rest to make up, and that, even at the best of times, sleep always attracted him. If he thought any more about his suspicions, he gave no sign. The others slept, too, when they could, for there was little else to do and no kind of distraction from their thoughts. But they spent more waking hours than Tobias, and often sat moodily in the little, ill-lit sitting-room, talking or remaining silent, according to their humours.

If Geoffrey had felt the subtle change in Tobias, he also felt a subtle change in Beatrice, and it puzzled him. During the first two days, she appeared aloof, and there were none of the little advances to which he had grown accustomed, and which he had also learned to fear. He feared them even more in this confined space, where one could hardly stretch without meeting some ornament or article of furniture, and the cooped spirit, fretting in its cage, was filled with volcanic longings. Thus, he was glad in his heart that Beatrice should be cold, while his mental faculties tried to find a reason for it, and his physical faculties rebelled. But, on the third afternoon, while Tobias was indulging in his usual siesta, she suddenly put down the impossible book she had been reading, and asked:

"Well, John, what is going to be the end of it all?"

"The end?" queried Geoffrey. "Is there such a thing? One merely passes from one stage to another."

"Very well, then, if you will have it so. What stage are we going to pass to next?"

"That's impossible to say," he answered, carefully. "It's largely in the lap of the gods."

"Don't talk nonsense," she exclaimed. "You've never left anything to the gods yet. You make your own plans. What are they?"

"You're right, Beatrice. I make my own plans. I have been making them all this time. And I think I begin to see daylight."

"Then you don't anticipate that we shall live in this wood for ever?"

"I don't." He smiled. "That would be hardly worse than going straight to prison, would it?"

"At least one can talk here. Prison? No—I'll never go to prison. That's why I asked you just now what was going to be the end of it. A bullet?"

A sudden vision of her end came to him—a vision of a beautiful woman with auburn hair and sweet, cruel eyes, and a revolver in her hand. He saw her at bay, with nothing but the revolver between her and Eternity. And he himself stood in the background, listening for the shot that would put momentary agony into those steady eyes, and reduce a graceful, breathing figure to a crumpled heap.

"John!" she cried, sharply. "What's the matter with you?"

"Nothing," he answered, coming to himself. "I was thinking."

"You look strange."

"Did I?" He laughed. "Well, we're in a strange position. I cannot tell you what the end will be, but I can tell you the next stage."

"I'm not interested in the next stage!" she burst out. "It's the stage after that I'm wondering about. Have you any settled plan about the future. Am I in it, and what part do I play in it?"

She spoke passionately, and there was a fierce light in her eye. Her very passion supplied him with the impetus to control his own, and he answered her in a steady, steely voice.

"How can I say? I do not look so far into the future as that. When every separate problem needs power and concentration, 'Sufficient for the day' is the motto I follow. Keep your eye on the mountain, and you will trip over a little stone in the road."

"Oh, drop metaphors! I'm serious. Look here, John—whatever happens, I'll not go to prison, or be captured, even. Do you know that?"

"It is exceedingly unlikely—"

"It's impossible!"

"Then why worry about it?"

She shrugged her shoulders, and suddenly changed her tone. "Well, let me hear about the next stage, then. What plans have you been hatching?"

"There are two things to be done in the immediate future. The first is to get out of this place—to re-establish our line of communication, so to speak, and reorganize our forces. The second is—to get that ruby. Money we must have, and I'm not going to let twenty thousand pounds go without fighting for it."

"Well! Go on!"

"We must make for Thrapley, our nearest head-quarters." He had learned this from Tobias, before the raid. "There we will be able to alter our appearances and get a change. Tobias, whose American accent I have tested, will leave us and eventually take rooms at the Regent Palace, booking extra rooms for his brother and sister—ourselves. We shall follow him in a couple of days, and, meanwhile, he will have got into touch with Lancing and others."

She nodded. "Yes, Arthur Lancing seems to have dropped out of things lately."

"He must drop into them again," said Geoffrey, and his mind harped back to that fateful afternoon in London when Arthur Lancing had handed him his "confession" with the rest. As he recalled the young man's pleasant features marred by a perverted mind, it came over him that his last captures might easily prove the most difficult of all.

"After this hole, a London hotel will be refreshing," proceeded Beatrice. "What shall we do there?"

"Enjoy the change for a short while, feel the pulse of things, and then go down to Littlehampton."

"Straight into the lion's mouth."

"The lion's mouth is often the safest place. But, of course, this is merely suggestive. We cannot decide anything at the moment. I want to have another search for that ruby, though, and perhaps, as American tourists, who will have visited the Morgue in Paris and the Chamber of Horrors, our curiosity when we learn of the Littlehampton affair may be naturally expected to lead us to the spot where the murder of James Cardhew took place. And it may even incite us to enter the place, in our morbidness."

Again she nodded. "Quite good, John. All the same, won't the police have searched the house?"

"Very likely. That we shall learn. But the police also searched the room at 22 Marine Row, and never found anything till I put them on the track."

"That's true. And—when we've got the ruby? How many will there be left to divide the spoils?"

"At this rate," he answered, promptly, "there may be only you and me. We shall have to lay our plans more carefully—in fact, I am particularly anxious to do so, because Tobias is ascribing his last narrow squeak to me. I daresay he has spoken to you about it?" She hesitated, and he rapped out, sharply: "Ah—he has?"

"Tobias is certainly not happy over it," she admitted.

Geoffrey Mordaunt smiled acidly. "For a wise man," he observed, "Tobias can sometimes be the most astounding fool."

Five minutes later the astounding fool came down, and beamed while he drank his tea.

A week went by. Plans were discussed and completed. And then a strange thing happened. Tobias went out for a morning stroll, and did not return.

It was on the morning of the day fixed for their departure. As the days wore on, their faces became more and more grave. At first they believed that some accident might have happened to him, and they scoured the forest for a mile around. But when their search proved fruitless, and he still did not return, they had to face two other more probable alternatives. The first was that Tobias had been caught. The second, that he had voluntarily decamped, for special reasons of his own.

Geoffrey combated the theory that he had been caught. He considered it highly unlikely, and told Beatrice so. Beatrice, on the other hand, could not reconcile herself to the idea of treachery, and argued that Tobias, whatever else he was, was not a rat.

"Then there is only one other thing I can think of," said Geoffrey. "It is that Tobias genuinely fears that I am a rat, and a rat to be avoided."

"Would you ever turn against your own kind?" she asked.

"No," answered Geoffrey, sincerely. "I would not."

"Tobias would need convincing on the point."

"So events indicate. But, tell me, my dear—hasn't Tobias ever said anything to you to suggest that, if the cheese were tasty enough, he might perhaps emulate a rodent?" He watched her closely, and noted the fact that she had no ready answer. "Anyway, he's gone, and we'll leave nothing to chance. He may have departed because he does not trust us. We will retaliate by showing that we do not trust him, and we shall be acting on the basis he himself approves of—mutual suspicion."

"Tobias is fond of me," replied Beatrice, "and would not do anything to harm me."

"That I believe," answered Geoffrey, "but there's no reason why we should not be on the safe side."

So that evening, in the guise of tramps, they set out in the woodman's cart, not for Thrapley, but for another small town in quite another direction. The woodman was a little anxious, but the prospect of finally getting rid of his burden made the risk worth while, and, as he said to his old woman when he got back, twelve pounds was twelve pounds, however you looked at it. And his old woman, praying to God for forgiveness, agreed.

CHAPTER 15

The Savoy was unusually full, and its after-theatre patrons were beginning to merge with the dancers and the resident guests. Reserved tables, gay with flowers, were rapidly appropriated, and immaculate couples who had not had the forethought to telephone through to the hotel in advance slipped swiftly into such unoccupied seats as were still available. And, meanwhile, the dance band, with the inextinguishable good-humour which is a dance band's stock-in-trade, lilted out its rollicking music above the tinkle of glasses and the hubbub of voices.

Presently eyes turned. Even in the midst of so much splendour, Miss Romack and her uncle always created something of a stir. It was whispered that old Mr Romack had made five millions dollars in a single month, and meant to hold on to it; but his niece, had she been penniless, would have attracted no less attention. Her lustrous bobbed hair, her Southern complexion, her flashing smiles, and the brilliant simplicity of her gowns, were of a nature to attract, and more than one visitor had prolonged his stay at the Savoy merely on her account.

So, many heads turned to watch them as they entered the hall and walked towards their table, and many hearts envied the young man with the scar who was with them this night.

Great as was the interest they aroused, it would have been a hundredfold greater had it been realized that the young man was Arthur Lancing, wanted by the police on many counts, that the beautiful girl was Beatrice Fullerton, the adventuress, and that the old man was the famous detective, Geoffrey Mordaunt, whose murder had recently been reported in the press. The onlookers would have been puzzled to account for such an odd assortment.

Suddenly Beatrice gave a low exclamation of annoyance.

"Look!" she murmured to the old man. "There's that odious young man again!"

"Say, so it is," squeaked Geoffrey Mordaunt. "What's he doing, sitting at our table?"

"I'd like to tweak his nose," said the young man with the scar, frowning. "He's done nothing but stare at us for two whole evenings."

"Us?" queried Mr Romack. "Not you and me, Mr Harland!" And he chuckled.

The young man at the table watched them approach, and went suddenly pink. He hesitated for a moment, and then summoned a waiter. There was a hurried conversation while the trio drew up. Then the usurper turned from the waiter, who stood by anxiously, and made a halting little speech.

"I'm awfully sorry," he stammered. "Seems there's been some silly mistake. I booked this table, too—and—well, there doesn't seem to be another seat anywhere."

The waiter advanced a step, and murmured something in the young man's ear.

"No, no!" protested the young man, still pink, but defiant. He turned to the others. "He says there's one seat empty, and wants me to sit opposite a fat negro! No, thanks! 'Pon my word, I'd just as soon go to bed, that I would!"

He smiled half-beseechingly. Arthur Lancing frowned.

"It's unfortunate," he said, shortly, "but Mr Romack reserved this table—"

"But—a negro, sir!" exclaimed the usurper, appealing to Geoffrey himself. "As an American—"

Geoffrey smiled.

"Well, well," he said, with humorous grace, "I can't say it's exactly in my heart to send you to that negro's table. Let's stay as we are, and introduce each other."

Geoffrey did not need any introduction himself, for he knew well who the young man was, and he secretly congratulated him on a disguise as effective as had been that of the horsy man at Brackleton, but he was interested to know by what new name Wilfred Hobson would call himself. Wilfred Hobson became appropriately pink.

"It's most good of you, I'm sure," he said. "Thank you very much—very much indeed. My name's Killick. I—er—I—er—hope you'll allow me to order the wine?"

"We'll be delighted, Mr Killick, delighted," replied Geoffrey, justifying old Mr Romack's reputation for enjoying lavishness at someone else's expense. "Edith, this is Mr Killick. Miss Romack, my niece. Mr Harland."

Stiff bows were exchanged, and the party took their seats.

There was a momentary silence, and then Wilfred Hobson became voluble. It might, to a casual onlooker, have been nervousness, it might have been a naturally talkative disposition, or it might have been that he had already given and disposed of one order for wine. Whatever the cause, that momentary silence was the last for a considerable while.

"You know, I can't bear negroes, never could," said Hobson, with a nervous little laugh. "As you're American, you'll agree with me, of course. It's a terrible question, sir, a terrible question!" He was addressing Geoffrey, but his eyes seemed to be interested chiefly in the girl, who had thrown back her cloak, and was regarding him with a half-amused, half-impatient expression. "Funny thing, isn't it, that Americans hate the negroes, yet they forced the negroes to go there—as slaves, you know. Ugh—and that big chap—there, look at him!" He turned and gazed in the direction of the portly black object of his loathing. "Don't wonder his table's empty. Would you sit there, sir?"

"I prefer my present company," answered Geoffrey Mordaunt.

The young man turned a shade pinker, before a new embarrassment swept over him.

"How silly I am!" he exclaimed. "I thought you meant me first —but of course you mean your niece and Mr Barland—"

"Harland," came the correction.

"Oh, Harland, of course. Forgive me! Have you just been to a theatre, Mr Harland?"

Theatres held the board for two minutes. Hobson suggested that Miss Romack ought to go on the stage. Then he suddenly jumped up, said he saw a friend he must speak to for a minute, apologized, and departed.

The trio watched him go, and then eyed each other.

"What on earth did you ask him to stay for?" demanded Arthur Lancing, in a low voice.

"It was rather foolish," agreed the girl.

"You think so?" retorted Geoffrey. "Well, it can't be helped now. And it generally pays to be courteous. It's going to pay for our wine tonight, my dear!"

"I'd rather pay for my own," she asserted.

"You mean, you'd rather *I* paid for it?" chuckled Geoffrey. "Well, listen here. I'm not sorry to be saving something. This trip is costing us quite enough dollars, as it is,"

He gave them a warning glance as Hobson darted back again.

"You'll laugh!" he cried, almost before he sat down. "My friend's looking for a house—oh, p'raps you don't know. There's an awful shortage about here. Too many people, and not enough houses to put 'em in." He smiled vapidly, and helped himself to caviare.

"You were saying—?" queried Geoffrey.

"Was I? Oh, yes. I was saying that my friend's trying to get a house. He can't get one anywhere." Again the caviare absorbed him.

"I can't see the humour of it yet," remarked Beatrice, rather witheringly.

"Humour? Oh, of course! I forgot. Well, what do you think? He's been offered a house where a murder's been committed." He leaned back in his chair and chortled. Then he suddenly became serious again. "Oh, but you don't know. The rich humour of it is that my friend is as nervous as a chicken."

"And did he take the house?" asked Beatrice.

He looked at her, reproachfully.

"Now, you're laughing at me," he said. "Well, p'raps it's not funny. No, of course he didn't take the house."

"Where is this sinister house?" asked Geoffrey.

"I don't know. Somewhere down Littlehampton way. No one'll go near the place because of the murder, they say."

"And who was murdered there?" asked Harland.

"Haven't the ghost of a notion. But I daresay I could find out from my friend. I never read about these things. I prefer cheerful things. Don't you?" He turned to Beatrice. "I wonder if you'd give me a dance. Would you?"

She regarded him. He looked wonderfully anxious.

"The next dance," she said. And he beamed.

"I'm rather interested in that house," remarked Geoffrey Mordaunt. "Where's Littlehampton? On the south coast? It might suit us, eh, my dear?"

Hobson became visibly agitated. His one object, apart from that of eating, appeared to be to serve his new friends, and he leapt in upon Geoffrey's suggestion like lightning.

"Do you mean that?" he exclaimed. "Well, I can get full particulars from my friend. He says the place is going cheap, because of its history—but I don't expect that'll weigh with you."

"It would weigh with me," answered Geoffrey, dryly. "There's a story that Rockefeller once disappointed a waiter through the smallness of his tip. 'If I was a millionaire, I'd be more generous,' said the waiter. 'If I were more generous,' replied Rockefeller, 'I might be a waiter.' Because a man has a pile of money, it doesn't follow that he wants to waste it."

"By Jove, that's *sense*," replied the young man. "Then may I see my friend again presently, and get the particulars for you?"

"I should be indebted to you," replied Geoffrey.

The meal continued, and presently, when the next dance began, Hobson rose in a flutter. Beatrice rose, also, to fulfil her promise, and the two of them made their way to the floor.

Geoffrey Mordaunt and his companion watched them go. The former smiled, Lancing frowned. It was evident that he was not at all happy over the turn taken by events. For some while, neither of them spoke. It was not until the first encore that

Geoffrey observed, with a cynical note in his voice:

"Jealous, my friend?"

"Oh, I've given up being jealous long ago," replied Lancing, in a low voice. "I wasn't thinking of that."

"Of what, then?"

Lancing shrugged his shoulders.

"The next three minutes may be the last you and I will have for private conversation for some while," said Geoffrey. "Pity to waste them, eh—if you've anything on your chest?"

"I don't like the way you're acting," answered Lancing. "It seems to me that you're heading full-tilt for disaster."

"How so?" asked Geoffrey. "We want an excuse to visit that house. We play our cards, and get into touch with a natural channel for attaining that end. Perfect safety, my friend, is impossible on this earth to—people like us. And, let me remind you, criticism is always fruitless unless the critic has an alternative policy."

"Well, I *have* an alternative policy. Quit this altogether, and launch some new scheme."

"And lose £20,000? I thank you, no."

"Some games aren't worth the candle."

"This one is. And I would like to know—Harland—what your particular objection is? We had the utmost difficulty to trace you. After getting out of our last tangle, and arriving in London in the guise of costers, we inserted our usual agony announcement, and you did not deign to turn up here till a week had gone by. But for Miss Romack—"

"Oh, why keep up that farce," muttered his companion. "We're alone."

"But walls have ears. But for Miss Romack, coupled with your own curiosity, we should not have traced you yet. It was her sharp eyes which spotted you when you crept here to observe and not be observed. It almost seemed as though you wished to disappear, like our mutual friend, Tobias King."

"Perhaps I did," returned the other. "Who knows? Your luck's dead out lately. Perhaps—like Tobias King—I'm not too eager to follow you."

"Nevertheless," purred Geoffrey, "you know me well enough, I imagine, to know that you now have no alternative. You know that you are being watched by one of my private spies, and that any attempt to escape would have very serious consequences. You will accompany us to Littlehampton, my friend, and that is all there is to say about it," He turned towards the returning couple as he announced this ultimatum, and smiled at them serenely. "How did the dance go?"

"She—she made me feel like thirty cents, as you say in America," exclaimed Hobson, enthusiastically. "I'm going to take dancing lessons right away, or she'll never dance with me any more."

"Say, Edith, he's not going to make me believe he's as bad as that," said Geoffrey.

"Mr Killick is too modest," she murmured, but her tone gave the lie to her words.

Presently, in the middle of eating an ice, Hobson darted away again with a muttered excuse. He concluded his business with lightning rapidity, and returned, flushed with triumph.

"I thought my friend might be going, and I only just caught him. Here's the address—Fir View, three miles from Littlehampton. I got the name of the chap who was murdered there, too. James Cardhew. The local agent will give you a permit to view the house."

"We'll go tomorrow," answered Geoffrey, "and it seems to me we owe you our thanks. I admire the way you've fixed this up, Mr Killick. We couldn't have done it quicker in America."

Hobson became immediately red and flustered.

"It must be your influence," he replied. "Anyway, I hope the place will suit you. But it would give *me* ten thousand jumps," Suddenly he exclaimed, as an idea struck him, "Look here, I wonder if you'd let me motor you down?"

"That would be presuming on your kindness," said Beatrice, quickly. "We couldn't think of it."

"Why not? I've got a car, and I've an aunt on the other side of

Littlehampton I've got to visit some time or other. I could drop you at the agent's—no going over that house for me, thanks!—and then pop round to see my aunt. And we could meet somewhere in Littlehampton two or three hours later, and then I could drive you back."

"That's very good of you," said Geoffrey. "It would be delightful. Only don't count on us for the return journey. We may stay down, or run along the coast while we're there."

"Then it's all arranged?" asked the young man, eagerly.

"I'm not sure that I could manage tomorrow," said Arthur Lancing, slowly. "That is," he added, in response to Hobson's look of surprise, "if I was included in the invitation?"

"I'm sure you were included," interposed Geoffrey, and turned to Hobson. "Mr Harland is with my party, you know." Then he turned to Lancing again, looking at him steadily as he spoke. "You're thinking of the Greens' invitation? Well, unfortunately, that's off. I had a wire this afternoon—we were invited, too, you know, and they asked us to let you know. So tomorrow is quite clear for all of us."

"Hooray!" cried the young man, ingenuously. "Now, there's only one thing left to complete my happiness. Another dance." And he looked, with humble beseeching eyes, at Beatrice.

She consented, again without any betrayal of enthusiasm, and Hobson stumbled round the room with her. The following dance was a tango, and "Mr Killick's" cup of happiness seemed a little dashed as he watched Arthur Lancing, in his place, put his art to shame.

"They make a good couple, eh?" chuckled Geoffrey, following them with his eyes.

"Yes, by Jove, they do," admitted Hobson, depressed. "I say, though. I can drive a motor all right, even if I am a muff at a dance."

"I'm not sure," returned Geoffrey, "whether you'd find yourself my niece's superior even in that!"

"Really?" murmured Hobson; and his gloom increased.

This was the last dance. The room had already half emptied,

and our party now rose, also, to go. Final plans for the morrow were made, eleven o'clock was agreed on for the start, and good nights were said.

Wilfred Hobson, his face expressive of bubbling happiness, sauntered out into the Strand, with a cigarette stuck jauntily between his lips. And the big black man, at whose table he had refused to sit, followed him.

CHAPTER 16

When Wilfred Hobson rose next morning, to greet the fullest day that would ever come into his experience, he found a note waiting for him. It had evidently been delivered by hand, and he recognized the writing as Joan Heather's immediately. Quickly tearing the envelope open, he read:

"Can you come round to my room at once? I am waiting for you, and have news."

"And so have I news—for her!" he thought, as he made his hurried toilet and hastened out into the street. He hailed an early morning taxi and, ten minutes later, found himself in Joan's presence.

"By Jove!" he exclaimed, as soon as he saw her. "You look dead beat!"

"I am a bit tired," replied Joan, smiling. "I've been travelling all night."

"Do you mean you caught the last train from Liverpool?"

"Yes, the 11.50, and got back here a little after six."

"Well, I won't say you ought to be in bed, Miss Heather, because you've evidently got something important to tell me first. But, as soon as I leave, I hope you'll see to yourself, and sleep all round the clock."

"I won't be able to help it," she laughed. Then she grew suddenly serious. "Well—I've traced them."

"You have? Where to?"

"Scotland. They're in Stirling at this moment. Read this. It's from a local paper, dated two days ago." And she handed him a news-clipping.

"The annual Flower Show opened in brilliant weather," ran

the report, "and a highly successful week is promised, if the attendance on the first day counts for anything. Among those present were Lady Blackie, Mr and Mrs Hepworth-Jones, Major Trant, and the American magnate, newly arrived on our shores, Mr J. P. Romack, and his niece."

"By Jove!" exclaimed Wilfred Hobson, with a glint of triumph in his eye. "That clinches it!"

"Here's another cutting," said Joan, taking it up and reading. "'Our representative was successful in obtaining a few words with Mr Romack, who is a most interesting personality. He said that this was his first visit, and that he had not come to Europe to spend money. He added, with humour, that he feared London would run away with too much of his wealth, so at the last moment he had decided to hide himself in the North, where he understood people were of a more saving disposition. He had actually booked his rooms at the Savoy, but had cancelled them by wire.'"

"My dear Miss Heather, this is splendid!" cried Wilfred. "Your work has just put the crown on my own. When I got ideas about that black man, and hung on to him, I felt sure he would lead me to my quarry—but, upon my soul, Miss Heather, the make-up of that old sham at the Savoy and his daughter is so wonderful that I couldn't be certain. All I could do was to stick close, make an utter ass of myself, and wait for the confirmation that you have supplied. Tell me, how did you trace those reports?"

"I made enquiries in Liverpool, and at last found the hotel he had put up at for the night. It wasn't one of the most expensive hotels—Mr Romack seems to be as mean as his reputation. They thought that he had gone North, but couldn't be sure, till one of the maids said she had heard Mr Romack mention Edinburgh. I ordered all the local papers circulating in Edinburgh, Glasgow and Stirling, and spent hours going through them. I came upon these notices last night, and returned at once to tell you."

"You've done better work than you imagine," replied Hobson. "I fixed up with the party late last night to drive them to Littlehampton. The old man nibbled my bait like a real hungry fish, and they're going over James Cardhew's house to see if it will suit them." He paused, with a grim smile. "Believe me—*it won't!*"

"Aren't you taking a big risk, Mr Hobson?" she asked, with anxiety in her voice.

"No bigger than Geoffrey Mordaunt himself would have taken," replied Hobson, soberly. "Yes, of course it's a risk. Everything is in this game. But it's got to be taken, for they'll have to be watched all the way, and I'm the one to do it. I'm handling this affair, Miss Heather—they're trusting me at head-quarters —and I'm going to see it through."

"Why don't you arrest them all before you start?"

"Because I'm playing for a big coup. We won't get the full gathering of the clans this end, in my opinion. At Littlehampton we stand our biggest chance of getting the lot—and, also, I want to find that ruby yet. If we don't disturb the nest too soon, I've an inkling we shall see some interesting developments down at Littlehampton."

"Well, good luck," she said. "I almost wish I were going with you."

"Personally, I'm jolly glad you're *not*," he laughed, in response. "You've done your bit, and it's your turn to rest. I hope, by the time you've slept all round the clock, I'll be back with good news. Well—hang that blackguard yet!"

"I can't help hoping you will," answered Joan, gravely.

The remark did not make Wilfred Hobson shudder. It merely showed the depth of her wound. Tired and weary, and very much alone, she appeared to the young detective a very pathetic figure. He wondered whether the memory of Geoffrey Mordaunt would ever fade, and whether she would one day allow someone else to give her the comfort and protection she needed.

"Take care of yourself," she said, holding out her hand. "You have been a very good friend to me, and if anything happened to you—"

"Nothing will," he assured her, taking her hand. "Have no

fear."

But his face was grave as he left her and returned home to don a light wig and transform his features into those of a vapid, well-meaning, and amorous young man.

CHAPTER 17

Geoffrey Mordaunt sat in a comer of the Savoy lounge, puffing a cigarette. Matters were coming to a head, and today, he felt, they would reach a climax.

In spite of the dangers around him, and in particular the riskiness of the impending trip to Littlehampton, he was bound to confess that matters were progressing well. As he thought over the events of the past few days—of the escape of himself and Beatrice from Brackleton, the journey to London disguised as costers, and then the successful impersonations of Mr Romack and his niece, a sense of completeness filled his professional soul, and he congratulated himself on having done all that humanly could have been done. He had succeeded in re-collecting the scattered fragments of his little force, and had put Wilfred Hobson on the track. He had even planted in Hobson's mind the seed of doubt that had sent Joan up to Liverpool to look for the authentic Mr Romack. His soul should have felt at peace.

But there was another soul in him, an unprofessional soul, and this was restless and ill at ease. Half a dozen criminals, including some of the cleverest in the land, had been brought to book through his manoeuvring, and more were to follow before the sun set again. But the prospect of delivering up Beatrice Fullerton, black though her record was, disturbed him uncomfortably. He told himself that this was, not because she exercised any attractions over him, but was the result of a close collaboration which, although the work was not of his choice, seemed to impose some sort of obligation, to be open to the meanness of treachery. He knew that he was being a traitor, within narrow limits, for the sake of a greater cause, and he felt no pangs of remorse for those who had so far fallen into his net. With Beatrice Fullerton, however, a different element seemed to enter. Was it merely her sex, he asked himself. Or was it something a little deeper?

"Uncle Romack, you're frowning," said a voice by his side.

He recovered himself swiftly, and smiled at the speaker.

"This is going to be an important day, Beatrice," he replied.

"Very. All the same, it isn't usual for you to be disturbed. What's on your mind?"

"Nothing," he answered, evenly. "I am not disturbed."

She studied him quizzically. Even with her shortened, darkened hair and somewhat aggressive dress, she looked wonderfully at-tractive. Suddenly, she gave a low laugh.

"John," she said, "I have discovered something about you."

"What is it?" he asked, coolly, though his heart gave a leap.

"You think me beautiful."

"That should be no discovery. Have I not always given you your due?"

And he smiled at her in his old acid way. His momentary fear that her discovery was more important had departed.

"No, you have not," she responded. "This is the first time that you have ever looked at me—like that."

"When I looked at you—like that—I was not looking at you at all. I was looking far beyond you, at a ruby."

"I have made another discovery, John," she answered. "There are times when you can lie quite badly."

He changed his tactics.

"Very well, my dear," he said. "Perhaps I was admiring you. But I can assure you of this. My thoughts were very different from those you imagine. You could never guess them."

She shrugged her shoulders, and her lips curled slightly. She appeared on the point of making some retort, but desisted.

"Lancing's here," she said, abruptly. "In a very bad temper, too."

"Lancing needs watching," he answered. "I've noted his attitude. We may have trouble with him."

"Why did you insist on his accompanying us on this trip?"

"Because, for the moment, I prefer Lancing right under my nose."

After a pause, she asked:

"Having him watched?"

"Of course."

"By whom?"

"That is my secret."

"Not yours alone, my good friend. I know who is watching Lancing."

"You do?" asked Geoffrey Mordaunt, interested. "Who?"

"Nobody," she shot out.

"Quite right," he replied. "You have lost none of your shrewdness. I had to bluff him about it."

She nodded. Then, suddenly, she laid her hand on his sleeve.

"John," she said, earnestly, "what is going to be the end of today's expedition?"

There was something curiously tense in her look, and he hesitated before replying. Her eyes were close to his, and seemed to burn into his soul. Her face was so near, as she bent towards him, that he could almost feel her breath upon his cheek. A delicate fragrance fought with his steadiness of purpose.

"I hope you're not losing your nerve, my dear?" he asked, hoping that he was not losing his.

She drew away from him, and, the next moment, she rose. An eager figure was approaching.

"Ah, there you are," cried Mr Killick, extending his hand. "This is splendid. I met your friend, Mr What's-his-name, outside, and he's by the car. It's a jolly day for our little run."

Geoffrey rose quickly, glad of the interruption, and took the young man's out-stretched hand.

"You're right, Mr Killick," he exclaimed. "Say, this climate of yours seems to have been underrated." And, while he spoke, he was thinking: "Wilfred Hobson, you're a genius—I never knew that a perfectly sensible young man could make himself appear such a vacuous fool!"

A few pleasantries were exchanged, and then the party trooped out into the courtyard, where a bright yellow car was waiting for them. Harland, frowning heavily, was standing by the car. When Mr Killick invited him to take the front seat, by the wheel, he hesitated for a fraction of a second Then, with a shrug, he stepped in.

"And now, if you'll take the back seats," said Mr Killick, bubbling with importance, "we'll start off. I've brought plenty of cushions," he added, with an adoring glance at Beatrice, "because I want you to be comfortable. Now, is there anything else you can think of?"

"Nothing," replied Geoffrey. "You seem to have provided for everything, Mr Killick."

The young man smirked, and started the engine. Whatever imperfections he may have betrayed in his nature, his conversation, and his dancing, it soon became clear that there was one subject he was master of. He was at home inside a car. He manoeuvred his car out of the court-yard and into the Strand with surprising skill, and did not attempt to keep up any flow of conversation while threading his way through motor-buses, taxis and carts.

After a few minutes, however, he warmed up, and began chatting with Harland, by his side. Harland's responses were mainly monosyllabic, but Mr Killick was not disturbed over that, for he had evidently set out to have a good time, and his attitude suggested that he was having it. Every now and again he threw a remark to the two occupants of the back seat, cracking jokes, and behaving something like a schoolboy on a spree.

"My aunt will get a big surprise when I walk in upon her," he exclaimed, as they ran through Clapham. "I visit her about once a year, just to please the mater. She's all right, you know, but a bit of a bore."

"Referring to your aunt?" asked Beatrice, politely.

"Well, of course," replied the young man. "You don't suppose I'd talk that way about my mother, do you?"

"Where is your mother?" enquired Beatrice.

Mr Killick did not reply immediately. He was swerving round a vegetable cart without slackening speed, and it required all his attention. Then he said:

"My mother? Oh, she lives in Nottingham. We've got a place there."

"But you prefer London?"

"Well, rather. Who wouldn't? Besides, my work's here. I'm a journalist, you know."

"And do you write under your own name?" asked Geoffrey, smiling. "Or do you prefer to perform your deeds under a bushel?"

"Oh, I use a *nom de plume*," answered Mr Killick, promptly. "You see, I write such awful stuff."

"But you must make something out of it," observed Harland, "if you can sport a motor-car."

"Good gracious!" laughed Mr Killick. "You don't suppose I run my motor on my articles? I run it on my late father's soap."

"He's an amusing young man," whispered Beatrice to Geoffrey. "But what do you really think of him?"

"Just the same as you do," replied Geoffrey. "Amusing."

They were approaching Ewell when suddenly those sitting behind the driver noticed his back stiffen. It was only a momentary action, but it was very distinct to observant eyes. They looked for the cause, and soon found it. A little way ahead, another car was preceding them—a dark red car driven by its solitary occupant, a big black man.

The dark red car was slackening speed, and they were overtaking it.

"See that?" said Mr Killick, recovered from his shock. "There's our pasty black friend of last night. Watch me show him our heels!"

The yellow car emitted its full ferocity of hideous sound, and the dark red car drew in towards the left side of the road. Then the yellow car flashed by, and gathered speed. The black man watched them go by, and his jaws snapped. He gave his own car more petrol, and followed in their wake.

Epsom was passed, and Leatherhead. Presently Beatrice asked:

"What time shall we get to Littlehampton?"

"In time for late lunch, if you like," answered Mr Killick, "or we can have lunch on the way—say at Horsham—and then get to Littlehampton at about three. What about that?"

"That'll suit us," replied Geoffrey, amiably, "We're not particular."

Their plans, however, were not destined to be fulfilled. A mile or two beyond Dorking, while Mr Killick was going at a good speed, the metallic purring of a powerful engine behind them fell upon their ears. The car behind, evidently, was going in for speed, too.

Mr Killick shot a glance back, and a shadow passed across his face. He increased his speed, but the motorist behind him did not appear anxious to be shaken off. A sudden tenseness tightened the atmosphere, and for a couple of minutes no word was spoken.

Then Mr Killick murmured:

"Looks to me as if that fellow's trying to race us."

"Why not let him?" suggested Harland.

"It's the black feller," continued Mr Killick. "I expect he's huffy, because I passed him. Well, I'm always on for a race, but not when I've got passengers."

"Yes, I think it would be wise to slow up," said Beatrice.

Mr Killick, though he tried not to show it, was plainly worried. Geoffrey Mordaunt was hardly less so. He knew that things were happening, that pre-arranged plans were going astray, and he held his mind ready for any emergency which might not only upset his own calculations but spell danger to Mr Killick. Perhaps the dark red car would merely take advantage of the slackening of the yellow car to pass it. Geoffrey's instinct told him, however, that this was highly improbable, and that the occupant of the dark red car had some deeper intention. And then, in a flash, he knew that the dark red car would not pass them, and he said to Beatrice, in a quiet voice:

"Look out!"

"What's happening?" she asked.

Their car was slowing up, and drawing into the side. A ditch lay between them and the hedge. They swerved perilously close to the ditch.

"He's not giving you much room," remarked Geoffrey.

Mr Killick grunted. They were obviously being "squeezed" into the hedge, and the big black man seemed very determined. Of the two alternatives of a collision with the oncoming car and the hedge, Mr Killick chose the latter. In another second, with a groan of abruptly applied brakes, the yellow car sidled into the ditch and came to a standstill.

"The fellow's a fool!" exclaimed Killick, as he picked himself up. "I say, are any of you hurt?"

Harland had been thrown out, but had fallen in soft grass, and was none the worse for the accident. Geoffrey and Beatrice were still in the car, but now they quickly clambered out and examined their scratches. The car itself, apparently, was the only serious casualty.

"Very nicely done," said Geoffrey. "I've never seen a prettier accident in my life. You certainly know how to drive, Mr Killick, and you keep your head."

"Thank you," murmured Mr Killick. "Good thing no bones are broken. But—we're in a bit of a mess, what?"

He looked genuinely distressed. His blithe spirits had received a nasty check.

Some way up the road, the dark red car had come to a halt, and the black driver had alighted and was coming towards them. He did not seem in the least perturbed, but he looked duly apologetic.

"Ah'm real sorry!" he said, as soon as he was within hail. "Is anyone hurt?"

"No one is hurt," replied Geoffrey, studying the black man. "And small thanks to you, sir!"

"The lady?"

"I'm all right," answered Beatrice. "But, as you see, the same can't be said of our car"

"Deah me!" mumbled the negro. "That's bad. Ah'm real sorry!"

"What the devil is the use of being sorry?" Mr Killick burst out. "You might have killed us all with your carelessness."

"Ah *was* careless," admitted the negro, blandly. "Real careless. Seems to me that car can't move no more?"

"And it seems to me that we'll have to give up our trip," said Beatrice.

"How far were you going?" asked the black man.

"Littlehampton," replied Beatrice.

The negro beamed.

"Well, well, for sure!" he exclaimed. "That's where Ah'm going, too. Say, the least Ah can do is to give you a lift?"

There was a moment's silence, while the idea welled into them. No one seemed particularly enthusiastic; on the other hand, no one seemed to find any logical words to veto the scheme. Littlehampton was their objective. Their car was *hors de combat*. To accept the offer seemed the obvious solution.

Suddenly, Geoffrey made up his mind. He nodded to the negro, and, turning to Mr Killick, said:

"If you're agreeable, Mr Killick, I think we might accept this offer. By doing so, we will relieve you of a burden, and—unless you want to accompany us all the way—we can drop you at the next place, wherever it is, and you can get assistance for your car."

Mr Killick nodded acquiescence, but he looked very depressed.

"I think I'll come to Littlehampton with you, though," he answered. "You see—there's my aunt."

"Why not telephone to your aunt?" suggested Geoffrey. "Any business you had to do in Littlehampton could perhaps be done over the 'phone?"

"That's true," exclaimed Mr Killick, brightening. "I *could* telephone. Yes, I'll tell you what. I'll come along with you, and then drop off somewhere if I want to."

"Sure," smiled the negro, and began to walk back to his car.

The late occupants of the car in the ditch followed him. There was nothing to do but to follow him. Their initiative had suddenly flown, and seemed to have become invested in this queer, bland negro who had run them down. In less than two minutes, they were purring along the road again, the negro and Mr Killick in front, and the other three behind. This time, Mr Killick was not at the wheel. He was a passenger.

Conversation flagged. Thoughts took the place of words. Each one would have given much to have known what each of the others was thinking, and had to suffice with conjecture. Mr Killick did make a brave attempt at conversation at first, but soon even he grew silent. Evidently his car, his aunt, or some other weighty matter, was beginning to get on his mind.

The primroses of Surrey gave way to the rusticity of Sussex. In the distance, the long line of the Downs loomed, dividing them from the sea. They caught a sudden unexpected glimpse of the rolling hills from the top of a steep climb, then lost them as they descended. A few miles before Horsham, Geoffrey Mordaunt spoke.

"Doesn't that car worry you, Mr Killick?" he said. "It would me."

"I don't like leaving it there," admitted Mr Killick.

"Then, if I were you," continued Geoffrey, "I'd drop off at the next town we pass through, telephone all your business to your aunt, and find a garage."

Mr Killick pondered. He was beginning to think this might be the wisest plan himself, and he could well understand, or so he imagined, why it was suggested to him. The black man, despite his peculiarities and mystery, was more in their line than Mr Killick was, and it was possibly occurring to various members of the party how particularly undesirable a companion Mr Killick happened to be on this trip. In that case, the outlook was grave. Yet, however grave the outlook, Mr Killick had no intention of relinquishing his mission. He would fulfil it, somehow or other. It was merely a question of ways and means.

The car in the ditch, he pondered, could wait. It would have to. But his aunt in Littlehampton—he could get into touch with her, and tell her, over the telephone, some very interesting things. But suppose, when he left the car, the party changed their plans entirely? It was this thought that made him hesitate. He believed that they would not change their plans. Mr Romack had impressed him with this belief. Still, there was the possibility, and the black man was the unknown quantity.

The black man, indeed, was a very real enigma. It was through knocking up against the black man a few days ago, and sticking to him like a leech, that Mr Killick had found his way to the Savoy and to the people he most wished to meet. Thus far, the negro had unconsciously performed him a very real service. But why was the negro himself acting so oddly? What was his game? That, Mr Killick admitted, baffled him entirely.

Geoffrey Mordaunt, watching Mr Killick's back, guessed at most of what was passing through that young man's mind. He had been keen enough, in the first instance, to have Mr Killick with them, for it fitted in well with his plans. The negro, however, altered the complexion of things. He had expected to meet the negro at some time or other, but not on the road to Littlehampton.

Suddenly, Geoffrey found himself watching the occupants of the front seat more closely. The negro had made some remark to Mr Killick, and Mr Killick had nodded. Slowing down slightly, the negro took a cigarette case out of his pocket, and gave a cigarette to Mr Killick. Mr Killick put it in his mouth. But, although twenty seconds later Mr Killick was quietly puffing smoke between his lips, Geoffrey noted that he was not smoking the negro's cigarette. He had contrived to substitute one of his own, and only Geoffrey's watchful eyes had detected him.

If Geoffrey had not detected him, he would have been seriously alarmed over an event which occurred a few minutes later. The negro suddenly turned in his seat, and asked his companion what was the matter with him.

"Don't know," mumbled Mr Killick.

"Feelin' ill."

"You'll soon feel better," said the negro, blandly.

"Hope so," murmured Mr Killick.

But the hope seemed a fragile one, for his distress grew. At last it grew too patent to be ignored.

"Want to be put down?" asked the negro. Mr Killick nodded.

"Don't know what's come over me," he said, faintly. "Put me down at the first inn we pass. I'll rest there, and you can go on."

They were passing an inn at that moment, but the negro did not stop. He affected not to notice another they came upon half a mile later. But, at the third inn, a small, evil-looking place on the outskirts of Horsham, he pulled up.

"Ah'll help you down," he said, assisting the dazed Mr Killick to rise. "You want a rest, that's what you want."

A greasy-looking man came out of the inn. A few whispered words passed between the greasy man and the negro, and Mr Killick was handed into the greasy man's care. Beatrice frowned slightly, and Geoffrey watched him disappear into the inn with tense eyes; but, beyond these unspoken signs, there were no expressions of regret at his departure. The negro, certainly, had no regrets, for he smiled very distinctly as he resumed his seat and put in the clutch.

Mr Killick, left behind, leaned heavily on the arm of the greasy man, and allowed himself to be led into a small room. Since the greasy man was clutching him wonderfully tightly, and a second greasy man was following in the rear, there did not seem any other alternative. Besides, he looked like a man on the point of collapse.

The greasy men exchanged glances. One raised his eyebrows. The other put his fingers to his lips. Mr Killick, though weak, had not quite lost his senses yet. Time enough—for anything—when he did.

Mr Killick sank into a seat. The greasy men left him. As soon as the door closed, a remarkable change came over Mr Killick. He recovered.

Gliding to the door, he was not surprised to find it locked. But the window, to a man in perfect health and strength, was an easy matter. In a trice he was out of it, had crept cautiously round the back garden and through a little gate, and was striding full speed for Horsham.

CHAPTER 18

Wilfred Hobson did not waste any time between the inn and Horsham, and during the latter half of the journey secured the assistance of a passing motor, but it was twenty minutes before he reached the police station, and he guessed that, by this time, the dark red motor must have covered a considerable number of miles.

He was recognized at the police station instantly, and preliminaries were dispensed with.

"I'll speak to you in a minute," he said, to the local superintendent, "but, first, I want Littlehampton."

"Right, sir," replied the superintendent, and the call was put through swiftly.

"Hallo," said Hobson.

"Hallo," said Littlehampton.

"Wilfred Hobson speaking. Who are you?"

"Grahame, sir."

"Good. The very man I want. There's an alteration in our plans. Now, listen."

"I'm listening."

"I shall not be arriving with our party, after all. Things went wrong on the road, and they tried to dope me. But, as you gather, they haven't."

"They got on to you, sir, then?" asked Grahame.

"One of the men did, but I'm not sure about the others. Anyway, that doesn't matter. Our strong point is that, if they do suspect, they believe I'm drugged. I imagine they are on their way to Littlehampton at this moment, and nearly there."

"What are your instructions, sir?"

"You mustn't wait for me, that's all. Otherwise, no alteration. Not a sign of you must appear until they are all in the house. Then, surround the house, and wait. Probably I'll be down myself before it's necessary to enter the house, for their search will take some time. The great point to remember is that we want them to have every chance to find what they're seeking before we catch them. I've a theory that that ruby will turn up some time this afternoon, and that there are wheels within wheels. Can't go into all that now, Grahame, but I just want you to bear it in mind. It's to be a waiting game."

"Yes, sir. I understand. But suppose it don't work out that way? Suppose our hand is forced?"

"Then you'll have to use your discretion. If necessary, you'll have to shoot. We're striking at the very core, you know—the cleverest and most unscrupulous brains in the whole concern. There can be no mercy, if it comes to that."

"What about the negro?"

"You needn't look out for him separately. He's with them. He's the fellow who got on to me. Whether he's told the others I can't say. He seems to have got some game on of his own."

"I'm glad you got clear of them safely, sir."

"Thanks. I'm not sure that I did right. I hated leaving them. But, if I'd stayed, I don't think I'd have had much of a chance, something would have happened to me between Horsham and Littlehampton, and they mightn't have turned up there at all."

"They still may not, sir."

"True, Grahame. But I think they will. And, as far as I can foresee, there are all the ingredients of as pretty a little bust-up, when they *do* get there, as their worst enemy could wish for."

Had Wilfred Hobson realized all the ingredients, he would have found it even harder to restrain his eagerness and keep a cool head.

"Is everything quite clear, Grahame?" he asked, finally.

"Absolutely, sir. I'll have my men posted. Where will you pick us up?"

"Have a man at the Greyhound, and keep him posted with

news. We'll leave our car there, and, if everything's in order, bring him along with us to the house. I think that's all."

"Yes, sir."

They rang off.

The Horsham superintendent, who had been standing by Hobson's side, chimed in.

"I've got the hang of it," he said. "No need for explanations. You'll be wanting to start at once."

"Yes," answered Hobson, "the less delay the better. You can spare half a dozen men?"

"Yes, sir."

"Good. I'd like them. I'm taking no chances this time, and too many are better than too few."

"That's right. They're getting the car ready. I hope you'll have good luck."

Hobson thanked him, and went out into the road. A large car, into which stalwart constables were tumbling, was already there. He regarded the men with satisfaction.

"I hope you're all going to assist in a fine afternoon's work, boys," said Hobson, as he stepped in himself, "and, if we're successful, I'll recommend you all for promotion."

The men laughed, and the car began its journey.

CHAPTER 19

The Turrets, a lonely grey-stoned house three miles from Littlehampton, had enjoyed many years of peace and uneventfulness before the murder of its last tenant, James Cardhew, had brought it temporarily into the limelight. It had been vacant for a considerable period previous to Cardhew's arrival, and the advent of the eccentric old fellow had not in any way added to its gaiety. Cardhew himself was as unapproachable as the house he lived and died in.

At first, he suffered a servant. Shortly before his death, however, he dismissed even her, declaring that she talked too much for his liking; and, if the servant had realized that the subsequent disaster was due to her talkativeness, she might have felt less aggrieved. For she discovered that her master was expecting a valuable ruby from abroad, and published the fact. But for this, no one would have known of it unless James Cardhew himself had desired.

The tragedy brought ephemeral fame to The Turrets, and curiosity-mongers walked or cycled or motored to the spot. There was so little to reward them, however, that they soon stopped coming, and for fully seven days before the afternoon on which it was destined again to find fame no one had been near the place. No human ear had heard the thick bushes rustle, no human eye had seen the slate that had been blown down from the roof in a wind-storm and now lay conspicuously before the front porch, and no human hand had opened or closed the gate that had swung to and fro in the wind.

But, on this afternoon, when the shadows were beginning to lengthen, and the blackened elongation of the tallest spire stretched almost to the bushes across the lawn, The Turrets found itself once more the centre of interest. A dark red motor drew up at the gate, the gate was opened, and the motor purred slowly up the curving drive. Then the occupants of the motor alighted—three men and a lady—and stood for a few moments, regarding the house, till the woman pointed to a window with a conveniently broken pane. At that, they all moved towards the window, an arm was inserted, the latch unfastened, and the window raised. And, in less than two minutes, the garden was deserted again, but for the incongruous motor; and footsteps went about the house. Not the ghostly footsteps of the past few days, but footsteps of the genuine, solid kind.

Shortly afterwards, there were two more visitors to the garden. When they saw the motor-car, they stopped and whispered to each other, and one of them retreated, while the other crept into the bushes. Then, the man who had retreated returned, with a dozen companions, and the bushes around the house became alive with eyes. And The Turrets realized that a page of rare interest was about to be written in its normally dull history.

"Before we begin," said Geoffrey Mordaunt, the last to enter through the window, "let us discard our mystery and our disguises. Why, Tobias, have you smeared your face so unnecessarily with brown?"

Tobias smiled, and his teeth gleamed with peculiar whiteness.

"Perhaps I will tell you the real reason later," he answered, resuming his familiar, placid treble. "Meanwhile, be content with the general fact that maybe I find it as necessary to disguise myself from the world of respectability as you."

"From the world—yes. But why from us?"

"*Did* I deceive you?" enquired Tobias.

"You deceived me," admitted Beatrice. "And you deceived Arthur Lancing."

The man with the scar nodded assent.

"Then my vanity is partially satisfied," said Tobias. "I could not expect to deceive the all-seeing eye of the great Chief."

"That is truer than you think," answered Geoffrey Mordaunt, quietly. "Nothing you have ever done has deceived me."

"And yet—you asked a question?"

"I ask many questions, with purpose, that I can answer."

The two men looked at each other, and the eyes of neither faltered.

"We're wasting time," exclaimed Lancing, impatiently.

"All the same," remarked Geoffrey Mordaunt, "I am willing to tell Tobias why he attempted to deceive us, if he wishes."

Tobias hesitated for a second. Then he said:

"My ears await thee, John."

"You tried to deceive us," said Geoffrey, smiling slightly despite himself—Tobias was certainly an amusing villain, "and you ran away from us, because you do not trust us. Your old, perpetual reason, Tobias. But, this time, you are more than usually alarmed. You are wondering, at this very moment, whether I am playing straight."

"He has spoken," purred Tobias, to the others. "Soon, maybe, I also shall speak. Meanwhile, our friend Arthur, whom no one would ever dream of mistrusting—eh, Arthur?—waits like patience on a monument. Shall we begin? I suggest that we start at the top, and work our way down."

The proposal was accepted, and the party moved out into the hall. The stairs creaked as they ascended, as though objecting to usage after their rest. The final staircase, winding round three sides of the wall, terminated in two garret-like rooms. Tobias and Lancing went into one, and Geoffrey and Beatrice entered the other.

For a minute or two, Geoffrey searched in silence, methodically and thoroughly, while Beatrice went somewhat listlessly to work. He tried not to notice her listlessness, but presently it forced itself upon him, and he stopped and looked at her.

"You haven't much hope?" he asked.

"None at all," she replied. "This is a wild goose chase."

"Very likely," agreed Geoffrey Mordaunt, as he glanced casually out of the window. "But worth the possible candle, eh?"

"I wouldn't mind giving it up!"

"I am sorry, my dear, that you do not share my own enthusiasm. You don't seem to realize what success will mean to us."

"What will it mean to us?"

"Well—twenty thousand pounds." He glanced at her. "Isn't that enough to fulfil our dreams?"

"Our dreams are not going to be fulfilled, John," she answered, with a little catch in her voice. "You believe it no more than I do. And—anyway—what *are* our dreams?"

"You have mentioned them often enough," said Geoffrey, fighting his uneasiness, and continuing with his search as he spoke.

"So I have. But are the dreams I have mentioned *your* dreams?"

"I'm ready to get out of all this, if that's what you mean."

"I wish, my dear man," she retorted, "that you were dead."

Geoffrey forced a laugh.

"As to that, my dear lady," he remarked, "we may both be dead before the sun sets if we don't hurry with our search."

"Yet, though I wish you were dead," continued Beatrice, as though he had not spoken, "I can't help warning you that you are in graver danger at this moment than you realize."

He stopped, and looked at her sharply.

"How do you know that I don't realize it?" he demanded. "I know perfectly well that, although we got rid of Mr Killick, the police may arrive at any moment. But we've got to take the risk."

"I'm not thinking of the police—I'm thinking of the men next door. Damn the ruby!" she burst out. "Why can't you let it rip?"

"Because," he replied, "I never let things rip."

"Then I advise you to make just one exception. Your record has been successful enough to satisfy anyone's vanity. Are you going to make the fatal mistake that brings so many strong men low? It's greed, my friend, that's what it is. Our prisons are filled with people whose one error has been that they have not known where to stop. Oh, I'd *hate* to see you bested! You may think what you like of me, but that's true. This may be our last chance of a talk together. We are safe, cooped up in this garret, but don't imagine that Tobias will have his eyes off you when we leave it."

"Bah! I'm a match for Tobias," he muttered.

"I'm not sure. Take my advice, John, and slip away. That's plain speaking, isn't it? Slip away, the first opportunity you get."

"And you?" he asked, curiously.

He saw her temptation, and saw her stifle it. "I'm not in your danger," she said, lightly.

Geoffrey did not reply immediately. He felt a great weakness creeping over him. He had known that this day would be difficult, but he had not realized how difficult. Again he glanced out of the window. The velvet shadows of the spires had by now licked their way right across the lawn below, and were pointing, like black arrows, into the bushes. Suddenly Geoffrey's gaze became fixed. He believed he had seen something stir in the bushes.

Beatrice watched him. He found her eyes upon him when he turned back to her.

"Well?" she asked.

He shook his head dully, while his heart began to stifle him.

"I'll not leave," he said, in a low voice, "until I find the ruby."

She went up to him, and, with her eyes still fixed on his face, asked:

"If the ruby is found—will you leave then?"

"Why not?"

"Why not!" she echoed, with an enigmatical smile. "Exactly. Why not! All the same, I would like to exact a promise from you. As soon as the ruby is found—if it is found—will you go?"

"I think there will be nothing to detain me."

"Damn you, John!" she exclaimed, stamping her foot. "You are the most exasperating man I ever met. If you won't promise. I'll go myself—*now*."

He turned once more to the window. Suddenly, she started. A new expression came into her face. What was her companion staring at, so fixedly?

"John," she said, sharply. "I'm going—*now*. This moment."

"You are not going, Beatrice," replied Geoffrey, coming away from the window, "for I promise."

She smiled, and her voice grew more natural.

"You've seen something, haven't you?" she asked. "You needn't hide anything from me," she added, as she saw him hesitate. "I've got pluck, you know, as well as you."

"I can't be sure, Beatrice," he answered. "I had an idea that something stirred in the bushes."

"Only an idea?"

"Yes, only an idea."

"Very well. Then we must hurry. There's a chance yet. We'll keep our idea to ourselves, and try and find that ruby before it materializes. Come along. I should think this room's about finished."

There were steps in the hall. Tobias looked in.

"No luck," said Tobias. "How have you got on?"

"Nothing," replied Geoffrey. "Let's move down now."

"Yes, and have a change of partners," chimed in Beatrice. "Perhaps our luck will change. Arthur, suppose you and I see what we can do together?"

For the first time that day, Arthur Lancing showed some sign of pleasure.

"I'm on," he said, and, making way for Beatrice, he slipped down the stairs after her. Tobias and Geoffrey followed. The arrangement suited Tobias admirably. The search continued.

Tobias and Geoffrey did not waste any moments in conversation. Apparently absorbed in their work, each covertly watched the other. Never had two men worked side by side with less trust. In another room, however, low voices were conversing freely, and Arthur Lancing's face was betraying an emotion of which few had imagined him capable. It was an emotion which, to do him justice, only a woman of Beatrice's power and attraction could have drawn forth.

"You mean it, Beatrice?" the young man muttered.

"Of course I mean it, Arthur," she replied. "I tell you, I'm sick of this game. For a long while now I've tried to get out of it. I want to try what being respectable is like—not because I'm really any more respectable than you are, Arthur, but because respectability, after all, does spell security and peace—and a time comes, doesn't it, when that hunted feeling gets on your nerves!"

"I know," said the young man. "That's true. Every day you get up may be your last!"

"Ah, you've felt it! I can see that. Every day may be the last. And, meanwhile, what do we get? Oh, I'm not saying that we get nothing. But there are some things we never get, and one is a full enjoyment of the money we earn. On the Continent—a long way off—it might be different. One could settle down, and enjoy life —with a companion."

"I don't understand you, Beatrice," replied Lancing. "You're such a devil, you know, and now it seems almost as though you're trying to play *me* up! I can understand your desire to live on the Continent—"

"I've desired it for years!"

"Yes, I've gathered as much. But your precious John had different ideas, and you've stuck to him. Why did you stick to him? How is it that you suddenly switch on to me?"

"I'll tell you," she answered, boldly. "I stuck to John because he seemed to me the person who could give me what I wanted. He has been the brains of all our enterprises. Oh, I've been attracted to him in other ways, too. But I'm through with him now. Lately, he has disgusted me. He will never make the break I want, his plans go awry—and there's something else."

Lancing was breathing heavily.

"One minute," he said, hoarsely. "Before you tell me that something else—have you ever been more than a friend to him?"

She was about to satisfy him with a denial, but suddenly she changed her mind.

"Never mind that," she replied. "You must think what you

like. Do you want to hear my other reason, or not?"

"Yes," he muttered. "Go on!"

"My other reason, Arthur," she said, slowly, "is this. I believe you have the means, quite apart from mere companionship, to satisfy my desires." He did not answer. "Am I right? Perhaps, if I am right, I can help you to convert the means into a comfortable instead of an uncomfortable possession."

"Sh!" whispered Lancing, looking fearfully towards the door. "Yes, you are a devil. How in thunder did you find out?"

"It was only a guess, Arthur—a guess based upon all that has happened, and a small piece of paper that I slipped out of your pocket in the motor-car. It's really time you turned respectable, you're getting so careless. Joe Flipp's hand-writing always was distinctive, you know. And the address on the paper of a certain individual who fakes precious stones, for a consideration, *did* make me think a bit."

Arthur Lancing's agitation grew.

"For God's sake, Beatrice, don't talk so loudly," he said. "Yes, you're right—and I'm glad you've found it out. Joe and I had the whole thing fixed up. Before he stole the ruby, we had another fake ruby made, and it was the fake ruby Joe passed on to Baxter in the salt-cellar. He gave me the real ruby that afternoon we all met in London—you remember, the day Geoffrey Mordaunt was killed—and we were planning how to vanish when Joe got caught. Then I got the wind up. You see, I didn't know how to get rid of the thing—"

"You needed the Chief's brains for that!"

"Ah, I admit it! I never realized till then how much we owed to him. But, you see, it was too late then, for, if I'd owned up. I'd have been done for. That ruby has been my curse. I've hardly slept a wink. Twenty thousand pounds, Beatrice—twenty thousand pounds! I couldn't let it out of my sight"—Beatrice gave an involuntary movement, but he did not notice it—"for fear of losing it, yet the one thing I longed for was to get rid of it."

"And you hadn't the pluck?" she asked, hiding her scorn.

"No, not with Joe caught, and the hangman waiting round

the comer! I went into retreat for some while, lost touch with things, and, even when I spotted the Chief's announcement and knew I was wanted at the Savoy, I kept away. But one day, as you know, curiosity beat me, and I went into have a look at your latest disguises. And I'd no sooner set foot in the place before I was spotted. Damn him! He misses nothing!"

"And then, of course, you had to stay?"

"Of course. He had me watched. He told me so." Beatrice smiled, and wondered what Lancing would have thought if she had told him that the Chief's spy had been a myth. "Well, that's over, anyway. You've opened the way for me now—for us—and, with your help, we'll get that ruby exchanged for good, solid cash, and then away to the Continent, eh?" He seized her hand, swept by his relief and his passion. "Beatrice—kiss me, just once! You devil! Just once, to seal our compact."

But she held him away.

"No, no, my friend," she replied. "Why should you have my kiss before I have my ruby?"

His hand dived impulsively into his breast pocket, but paused there. The door of the room had opened.

CHAPTER 20

When Geoffrey and Tobias entered the room, their attitude suggested important happenings. Beatrice regarded them coolly, but with a tumultuous heart. Lancing stifled his emotions with greater difficulty. No word was spoken while Tobias closed the door. Then Geoffrey made his announcement.

"This house," he said, simply, "is surrounded."

Lancing gave a gasp. He seemed momentarily incapable of speech, and it was Beatrice who asked:

"You are sure of that?"

"Quite sure. I was beginning to get worried myself, as you know, Beatrice—"

"You said nothing of that," interposed Tobias, sharply.

The tone was challenging. Geoffrey smiled.

"Beatrice and I agreed mutually that what we saw from the upstairs window was probably nothing but a breeze among the bushes—and probably we were right. It does no good, on an occasion like this, to jump at fancies. But now there are too many movements among the bushes, and Tobias declares that once he saw the distinct flash of a revolver."

"That is most unfortunate," replied Beatrice, calmly, "for it means we have been beaten only by the clock."

"What's that?" demanded Tobias, sharply, and Geoffrey's face lit up with sudden interest.

"Arthur Lancing has found the ruby," announced Beatrice.

There was a moment's silence. At that second, Beatrice was the only calm person in the room. Lancing's brain was in a turmoil of doubt and fear. He did not know where he stood, or how he was coming out of it. Geoffrey, to whom this announcement meant the final crowning of all his efforts, was momentarily dazed. Even Tobias, usually bland and unruffled, looked astonished.

"Damnation!" he cried, at last. "The ruby! And the cursed police outside!" Then he confronted Lancing. "Where is it?"

"In his pocket, of course," replied Beatrice. "When you entered the room so abruptly, he slipped it in. For all we knew, you might have been the police."

Lancing took advantage of the opportunity afforded him by Beatrice's explanation. He produced the precious stone, and Tobias gave a grunt of amazed satisfaction. But the next moment he was cursing again.

"Don't lose your head," suggested Geoffrey, regaining his own. "The game's not up yet. Well find a way out."

"Of course we will," said Beatrice. "Let's stop fuming, and discuss plans."

Tobias, however, did not appear to be in a mood for co-operation. He grew calmer, but his eyes blazed as he looked at his companions.

"Yes, we'll discuss plans," he answered, "but, before we discuss plans, we'll discuss explanations. Where did you find the stone, Lancing?"

"You're a fool, Tobias," retorted Beatrice. "The stone was found in that mouse-hole over there, but is this the time to talk over such points? They'll keep. Our one object now is to escape, with the stone. And there's one person here I'll trust to do it, and that's our Chief. I might have trusted you more if you'd kept your head better—and if you hadn't left us at Brackleton like a rat deserting a sinking ship."

Beatrice's speech, delivered with fire, had a sobering effect upon Tobias. He blinked round the room. Then he nodded, and spoke more in his old tone.

"You're right, Beatrice," he said. "Our one object now is to get away." He walked to the window, and looked out. "But as the police seem to be playing a waiting game—I see no sign of them—there is no need for us to act upon a hasty decision."

"My mind is already made up to one thing," said Beatrice, taking the ruby from Lancing, who made no protest. "The only brains to trust to in this affair are John's, and the only man who can be safely trusted with £20,000 in his pocket is John," She went up to him, and gave him the stone. Geoffrey took it from her, looking at her gravely, and slipped it into his pocket. "And now, John," she continued, "I suggest that we wait for you here, while you slip down and have a look around. What do you say, Arthur?"

"I agree," answered Lancing, ready to agree to anything at the moment.

"I am not sure that I agree, however," said Tobias.

"You!" exclaimed Beatrice, stamping her foot. "Tobias, there are times when I am very fond of you, but today you are nothing but an annoying child!" She turned to Geoffrey. "Go!" she said. "We will wait for you here."

"No, don't go," interposed Tobias, and, although Geoffrey had made no movement, he found himself suddenly covered by Tobias's revolver. "The annoying child is on the point of growing more annoying. You say you trust this man, Beatrice? And you, Arthur Lancing, are ready to trust him? Well, I do not trust him. I failed to respond to the summons in London because I did not trust him. I disguised myself in all this abhorrent paint because I did not trust him. I got rid of the fantastic Mr Killick because I did not trust him. I am, as you know, a most untrusting person. I have never hidden the fact. Have I, John? Why, I am even covering you at this moment, and will shoot you if you stir so much as a little finger, John, because I do not trust you."

"Stop this nonsense!" cried Beatrice.

But Tobias refused to stop it. Thorough master of himself once more, thoroughly cool and bland, he kept his revolver pointed at Geoffrey's heart with a hand that was firm as a rock, and a determination that was clear as crystal. Geoffrey knew that, if he made one false move now, he would be dead the next instant. He wondered whether he cared very much. It was only the sudden thought of Joan Heather, the sweet, unsullied girl, waiting for him unconsciously and ready to throw open the gates of happiness to his tired spirit, that kept him from careless rashness.

"You say nothing?" observed Tobias.

"Impatience is never one of my crimes, Tobias," replied Geoffrey. "I am waiting for you to say all you have to say first."

"Good. Then let me continue. I will tell you why I do not trust our Chief—though, understand, I am ever ready to love and cherish him again if I find him worthy of it."

"He has brought us to the ruby," Beatrice reminded him.

"True. And for that I am duly grateful. But under what conditions? How can we enjoy the fruits of what he has brought us to? Those bushes out there are full of eyes. Perhaps they merely await his signal, eh?"

"His signal!" exclaimed Arthur Lancing, in astonishment. "What in thunder do you mean?"

"I will address my remarks to you, my dear Arthur, for—although I trust you little—very little indeed, dear Arthur—at the moment you seem to be in greatest possession of your senses. You recall a certain day when a tramp came to our house in London? A nasty, dirty fellow, I never liked him. Our dear John went up to interview him, discovered him to be his brother, Geoffrey Mordaunt—you remember?—and killed him. Very proper, very proper. It was quite the right thing to do. I should like myself to have the distinction of having killed Geoffrey Mordaunt, the cleverest detective of his time. Nothing would make me happier. I would even risk my life to do it."

"Oh, get on," snapped Lancing. "Yes, I remember the day. Well, what of it?"

"After that day, Arthur, things began to go wrong. They went very wrong. Remarkably wrong. Our dear Chief planned his trip to Littlehampton, and we lost two valuable friends—Joe Flipp and Edward Tapley. Bear in mind these things, Arthur. And you, too, Beatrice, for they affect you as much—perhaps even more—than they affect Arthur and me. Well, to continue." The whites of his eyes gleamed unpleasantly against his rich brown complexion. "After Littlehampton, we foregathered in Brackleton. Beatrice and John picked up Baxter, *en route*, and I arrived in due course with a valuable hostage. And what happened in *Brackleton*? Again the police caught us napping. Baxter was taken. Jones —you recall Jones, whose money was going to be so useful to us, and whose brain might have helped, too, for we had marked him as a pretty fellow—Jones was taken. Mr Jowl was taken. The beautiful Mrs Jowl was also taken. And the only reason that I was not taken myself was because I am cleverer than Baxter, or Jones, or Mr Jowl, or the beautiful Mrs Jowl. Is it so surprising, Beatrice, that I made myself scarce at Brackleton, and left the wood-cutter's cottage like luggage in advance? I think not. I think not. The Chief's protecting cloak had not, you see, been spread over me as it had been spread over you."

"All this is true," admitted Arthur Lancing, looking at Geoffrey with a new interest. "But what the devil are you getting at? We all make mistakes at times. Are you accusing him of treachery?"

"Yes, we all make mistakes, but I do not think these were mistakes. Listen to me one minute more, and then I shall have finished, and you will advise me whether or not to put a bullet in our dear Chief. You, Arthur, were no more anxious to join forces with him again than I was. I won't enquire for the moment into your reasons, but I have explained mine. He contrived, however, to get us both into his clutches again. If I came voluntarily, for I was still attracted by the ruby, I'll wager he knew that I would come. He made up to Mr Killick, who was neither more nor less than a detective. I did my best to finish, off the detective, and gave him a drugged cigarette, and left him to get over the effects in good hands. But the Chief seemed anxious for me to leave Mr Killick at any wayside inn, instead of the inn which expected his coming. And, now, the house is surrounded, and Mr Killick seems to have got over that drugged cigarette. And I suggest to you, Beatrice, and to you, Arthur Lancing, that the reason for all these things is that the man at whose heart my revolver points is, not our dear John, but Geoffrey Mordaunt, the detective." Beatrice's hand went up to her breast, and Lancing started violently. "I suggest that Geoffrey killed John, not John Geoffrey, and that, even at the cost of capture, I should send a bullet into that man's heart."

"One minute, one minute!" cried Lancing. "All this is possible. It's too enormous to embrace all at once, but it's possible. Yes, things have been going queerly lately. But don't shoot yet. There must be some other way. If we're caught, we'll be hanged for murder. Let's hear what he has to say, and then, if we're not satisfied, truss him up and make a dash for it."

"Ah, now," came Geoffrey's cool voice, breaking into a short, strained silence. "perhaps I may be allowed a few words. Tobias's facts are right, but his deductions are wrong. The trouble has been, as I have told you all repeatedly, that we have been acting lately in a maze of suspicion, in a disjointed instead of a united way, in a spirit of envy and jealousy. Edward Tapley was jealous of my leadership, and he was jealous of my friendship with Beatrice. Tobias here, admittedly suspicious of me, nevertheless requires me to be unsuspicious of him, and to act as though I had no suspicion of him. He, too, is jealous of my position among you, and anxious to wear my shoes. Everyone, excepting Beatrice, has pulled away from me lately, and I have had no chance to organize our forces as I used to do. How, in these circumstances, could we hope for happy results? Why, even you, Lancing, have your private secrets, I doubt not, and have not acted straight with us in this search for £20,000. You came on this trip unwillingly. You tried to dodge me. Yet—have I not brought you to the very thing we sought?"

Tobias's fingers moved fretfully. At one moment, Geoffrey thought that the end had come. The atmosphere became tenser, and the patch of sunlight that shot through the window and turned a streak of carpet into a bar of gold looked unnaturally cheerful. But Geoffrey's words had had some effect. Tobias hesitated, and Lancing was plainly impressed by them. It was clear that Geoffrey's fate lay in the balance, and that a hair on either side would settle it.

Suddenly, as though waking from a stupor, Beatrice spoke. Her words rang clear and swift, and, while she spoke, Geoffrey stared at her with emotions which he found next to impossible to conceal.

"I will admit, Tobias, that you had plenty of cause for your suspicions," said Beatrice, in a quiet, even voice, "and, if what you thought had been true, I should be the first person to tell you to shoot—because, you see, by my peculiar relationship with John, I should have been the greatest sufferer. I have always hoped, as you know, to marry John one day. I speak openly, because, at moments like this, concealment can cost too much. But"—and here her voice contained its first slight tremor —"though John and I are not yet married, we have not waited for that day. If he were not John, Tobias, I should be the first person in the world to know it."

There was a silence. Geoffrey looked at Beatrice, and asked himself whether this was the woman he was about to give into the hands of the police, to subject to years of indignity and imprisonment, however richly they might be merited by her past deeds. Then Tobias said:

"Is this true, Beatrice?"

"Ask Arthur Lancing," replied Beatrice, steadily.

Lancing flushed. "Yes—I think it is true," he replied. "I, too, am fond of Beatrice, and she suggested to me—not more than ten minutes ago—that she and John were—more than friends."

Tobias nodded.

"A woman's love usually embarrasses a man," he said, reflectively. "In this case, John, it has been peculiarly convenient. My jealousy remains, but I am satisfied." And he slipped his revolver back into his pocket.

They waited for Geoffrey to speak. Beatrice alone understood the full measure of his emotion. A minute went by.

Outside, the police officials waited for some signal that he could give them. Inside, reinstated, he had his companions at his mercy. The ruby was in his pocket, the game won. Yet he hesitated.

"Well?" said Beatrice. "What are you going to do?"

"I am thinking," replied Geoffrey Mordaunt. "Wait."

Once before, in another room, he had had a man at his mercy, and through some strange instinct, logicless but human, he had given that man his chance. The man—his brother—had killed himself. These people before him now, fresh victims of his craft, were bound to him by no flesh and blood ties, they had no thoughts, no ideas in common, and they represented the evil, unfortunate elements it had become his creed to war against. Yet, once again, he found the position too big for him. He could not take advantage of the gift of their renewed confidence in him. His sense of stem duty snapped.

"Take out your revolver again, Tobias," he said. "You were quite correct. I am Geoffrey Mordaunt."

Tobias's revolver was out again in an instant, but he did not immediately raise it. The sudden reaction, following upon this unnecessary admission, beat him momentarily, and his one emotion was astonishment. Lancing, quite unable by now to act on his own initiative, watched Tobias for his cue.

"I ought not to make that admission," continued Geoffrey Mordaunt. "My duty is to my work, and my work is to trap such folk as you. But since Beatrice has taken it upon herself to defend me, at the expense of her honour, I find myself unable to accept her sacrifice. Therefore, inside this house, I give you your chance of pitting yourselves against me, if you wish to, on level terms. But, one moment," he added, as he noticed a glint in Tobias's eye. "Let me give you one word of warning. I give it in your interests, not mine. If you refrain from attacking me, I will stay here without interfering with any attempt you may make to escape. That concession you owe to Beatrice. On the other hand, if you do attack me, the best you can hope for is to kill me, and the result will inevitably be a rope round your neck. Your chances of escape, in either case, are absolutely negligible."

Tobias studied Geoffrey, and then smiled.

"You're a damned clever fellow," he said, with less malice than might have been expected, "and you'd have made a damned fine crook. I accept your offer. Remember, if we're caught, that I could have shot you if I'd liked." He paused. "But upon my soul, John—I should say, Geoffrey—I'm beginning to love you far too much." He turned to the others. "Well, shall we make our dash to liberty? The odd chance sometimes wins."

Lancing walked towards the door, but Beatrice did not move.

"I daresay you're wise, my dear," purred Tobias. "There's nothing like a friend at court."

The taunt went home. She jumped up at once. But Geoffrey called after her.

"Stay here!" he said, sternly. And she obeyed.

When the door had closed, and they were alone, he turned to her and asked:

"How long have you known that I was Geoffrey Mordaunt, Beatrice?"

"Since that evening at the wood-cutter's cottage," she replied, "when I bathed your knee. John's knee had a terrible scar. I knew, from that moment, that you were not John."

"Yet you did not give me away?"

"I loved John," she said, simply, "and you are very like him."

"I, too, loved John. We played together as boys. For all his bad deeds—and God knows how bad they were—I find myself loving him still."

"Yet you killed him!"

"No, I did not kill him. I gave him his chance to kill me, and he chose to kill himself. John's last act was a noble one." He saw that tears were glistening on her lashes—the first tears she had shed for years. "And your last act, my dear, has been a noble one, too."

"Well, don't expect me to go on doing fine acts," she exclaimed, fighting her weakness.

"I do expect it. I am going to give you your chance."

"My chance? What do you mean?" she exclaimed. "Have I really found a friend at court, then?"

He nodded.

"Of course, you have. Do you think I could send you to prison after the way you have acted? It would be impossible, inhuman. Perhaps I am deceiving myself. Perhaps I should set aside your good deeds, and think only of the bad ones. Well, I can't. I began by hating you, Beatrice, and swearing that I should not lie content in my bed till I had brought you low. But I feel differently towards you now. I know that, beneath all your hardness, your errors, your mistaken ideas, there is something womanly, and good. And I want, instead of bringing you low, to help, if I can, to raise you high. May I do so? May I help you to reach the Continent?"

Her tears were falling fast now. Through them, she asked:

"Why are you so interested in me?"

"Because you have proved your loyalty."

"If I were loyal, would I not be outside, with Tobias and Arthur Lancing?"

"You could not help them. They have no chance. Attach your loyalty, now, to something better, something nobler. There is always good work to do, Beatrice. You are fitted for better things than making mail-bags."

He walked to the window. The bushes had emptied themselves on to the lawn, now crowded with officials. Tobias and Lancing, realizing their hopeless position, had not wasted their substance in fruitless exertions. Their attempt to slip away had failed, and Geoffrey caught a glimpse of Lancing's sullen face and Tobias's resigned one. Even in defeat, Tobias could smile, and, while he smiled, could scheme.

Suddenly Geoffrey came away from the window. Wilfred Hobson was approaching the house.

"Beatrice," he said, abruptly, "you tried to help me just now. Let me make you some return."

"My dear friend," she replied, "I am in your hands."

"Good. Then take these notes." His tone was brisk, and he pressed a bundle into her fingers. "Remain here till night. Then slip away, and get to Folkestone or Dover as best you can. And after that, Beatrice, God help you, as I hope He will forgive me!"

He bent down and kissed her, feeling no disloyalty to Joan

as he did so. Then, leaving the room quickly, he ran down the stairs, and ten seconds later found himself covered by Wilfred Hobson's revolver.

"At last!" cried Hobson.

"At last!" replied Geoffrey.

The two men stared at each other. Then Geoffrey laughed.

"Your luck's out again, Wilfred," said Geoffrey. "Dead out. You'll never catch the man you're looking for."

"What do you mean?" demanded Hobson.

"I mean that I'd rather have your hand than your bullet, you dolt!" exclaimed Geoffrey. "I'm Geoffrey Mordaunt."

Six hours later, in a small, happy room in London, Geoffrey looked into Joan Heather's eyes and asked a question.

"Did I do right?" he said. "Did I do right to let her go?"

She squeezed his hand.

"I don't know," she whispered. "But in your place—I should have done the same."

And Geoffrey wanted no more.

J. JEFFERSON FARJEON'S CRIME NOVELS & SELECTED OTHER WORKS

The Master Criminal (London, Brentano's, 1924)

The Confusing Friendship (London, Brentano's, 1924)

Little Things That Happen (London, Methuen, 1925)

Uninvited Guests (London, Brentano's, 1925)

Number 17 (London, Hodder and Stoughton, 1926. A 'Ben the Tramp' Mystery)

At the Green Dragon (London, Harrap, 1926. US title: *The Green Dragon*)

The Crook's Shadow (London, Harrap, 1927)

More Little Happenings (London, Methuen, 1928)

The House of Disappearance (New York, A. L. Burt, 1928)

Underground (New York, A. L. Burt, 1928. Alternative title: *Mystery Underground*, 1932)

Shadows by the Sea (London, Harrap, 1928)

The Appointed Date (New York, A. L. Burt, 1929)

The 5.18 Mystery (London, Collins, 1929)

The Person Called 'Z' (London, Collins, 1929)

Following Footsteps (New York, Lincoln MacVeigh 1930)

The Mystery on the Moor (London, Collins, 1930)

The House Opposite (London, Collins, 1931. A 'Ben the Tramp' Mystery)

Murderer's Trail (London, Collins, 1931. US title: *Phantom Fingers*. A 'Ben the Tramp' Mystery)

The 'Z' Murders (London, Collins, 1932)

Trunk Call (London, Collins, 1932. US title: *The Trunk Call Mystery*)

Ben Sees It Through (London, Collins, 1932. A 'Ben the Tramp' Mystery)

Sometimes Life's Funny (London, Collins, 1933)

The Mystery of the Creek (London, Collins, 1933. US title: *The House on the Marsh*)

Dead Man's Heath (London, Collins, 1933. US title: *The Mystery of Dead Man's Heath*)

Old Man Mystery (London, Collins, 1933)

Fancy Dress Ball (London, Collins, 1934. US title: *Death in Fancy Dress*)

The Windmill Mystery (London, Collins, 1934)

Sinister Inn (London, Collins, 1934)

The Golden Singer (London, Wright & Brown, 1935)

His Lady Secretary (London, Wright & Brown, 1935)

Mountain Mystery (London, Collins, 1935)

Little God Ben (London, Collins, 1935. A 'Ben the Tramp' Mystery)

Holiday Express (London, Collins, 1935)

The Adventure of Edward: A Light-Hearted Romance (London, Wright & Brown, 1936)

Thirteen Guests (London, Collins, 1936)

Detective Ben (London, Collins, 1936. A 'Ben the Tramp' Mystery)

Dangerous Beauty (London, Collins, 1936)

Yellow Devil (London, Collins, 1937)

Holiday at Half Mast (London, Collins, 1937)

Mystery in White (London, Collins, 1937)

The Compleat Smuggler (London, George G. Harrap and Co 1938)

Dark Lady (London, Collins, 1938)

End of An Author (London, Collins, 1938. US title: *Death in the Inkwell*, 1942)

Seven Dead (London, Collins, 1939)

Exit John Horton (London, Collins, 1939. US title: *Friday the 13th*, 1942)

Facing Death: Tales Told on a Sinking Raft (London, Quality Press, 1940)

Aunt Sunday Sees It Through (London, Collins, 1940. US title: *Aunt Sunday Takes Command*)

Room Number Six (London, Collins, 1941)

The Third Victim (London, Collins, 1941)

The Judge Sums Up (London, Collins, 1942)

Murder at a Police Station (London, Hale, 1943, under the pseudonym Anthony Swift)

The House of Shadows (London, Collins, 1943)

Waiting for the Police and Other Short Stories (London, Todd Publishing Co, 1943, a short story collection)

Greenmask (London, Collins, 1944)

Black Castle (London, Collins, 1944)

November the Ninth at Kersea (London, Hale, 1944, under the pseudonym Anthony Swift)

Rona Runs Away (London, Macdonald, 1945)

Interrupted Honeymoon (London, Hale, 1945, under the pseudonym Anthony Swift)

The Oval Table (London, Collins, 1946)

Peril in the Pyrenees (London, Collins, 1946)

The Invisible Companion and Other Stories (London, Polybooks, 1946, a short story collection)

Midnight Adventure and Other Stories (London, Polybooks, 1946, a short story collection)

The Works of Smith Minor (London, Jonathan Cape, 1947)

Back To Victoria (London, Macdonald, 1947)

Benelogues (no publishing information 1948)

The Llewellyn Jewel Mystery (London, Collins, 1948)

Death of a World (London, Collins, 1948)

The Adventure at Eighty (London, Macdonald, 1948)

Prelude To Crime (London, Collins, 1948)

The Lone House Mystery (London, Collins, 1949)

The Impossible Guest (London, Macdonald & Co, 1949)
The Shadow of Thirteen (London, Collins, 1949)
The Disappearances of Uncle David (London, Collins, 1949)
Change With Me (London, Macdonald & Co, 1950)
Mother Goes Gay (London, Macdonald, 1950)
Cause Unknown (London, Collins, 1950)
Mystery on Wheels (London, publisher nk 1951)
The House Over the Tunnel (London, Collins, 1951)
Adventure For Nine (London, Macdonald & Co, 1951)
Ben on the Job (London, Collins, 1952. A 'Ben the Tramp' Mystery)
Number Nineteen (London, Collins, 1952. A 'Ben the Tramp' Mystery)
The Double Crime (London, Collins, 1953)
The Mystery of the Map (London, Collins, 1953)
Money Walks (London, Macdonald, 1953)
Castle of Fear (London, Collins, 1954)
Bob Hits the Headlines (London, Bodley Head, 1954)
The Caravan Adventure (London, Macdonald 1955)

Serialised Short Fiction

Between June 1925 and April 1929 Farjeon's fictional reformed criminal turned private detective *Detective X. Crook* appeared in over fifty issues of *Flynn's Weekly* one of the most popular, and longest running, of all the detective pulp magazines.

Plays

Number 17 (1925)
After Dark (1926)
Enchantment (1927)
Philomel (1932)